The Undercover Cowboy

The Undercover Cowboy

A Sweethearts of the Rodeo Romance

Jamie K. Schmidt

TULE
PUBLISHING

Chapter One

Dolly Keller

DOLLY KELLER'S PERFECTLY manicured nails tapped away at her smartphone screen, while her eyes scanned the chaotic scene of the opening day of the United Professional Rodeo Circuit rodeo's season in Killeen, Texas. She hoped this year would be better than the last one, for all their sakes.

Leaning up against a dusty, weathered wall of a nearby barn, Dolly was aware of the cowboys trying to get her attention. As the head of social media for the UPRC, she oversaw the social media accounts of the rodeo and its athletes, including Nash Weaver—a terrible bull rider who made her job far more challenging than it needed to be. To be fair, though, he wasn't a real cowboy. He was a retired FBI agent who was helping his sister nail her partner for fraud or something RICO-related.

Her thumb hesitated over the "post" button. Dolly wanted one last look at the portrait of Nash she had edited. His muscles taut as he gripped the reins, Nash was a study in concentration and grit. The sepia filter gave the photo a timeless quality, which would hopefully obscure the fact that his recent performances had been less than legendary.

"It's a good thing you're sexy as hell," she murmured. "Because you can't ride for shit."

Nash's sister, Shelby Miller, the former president of the Women's Professional Rodeo Circuit and Jackson Blevins, former head honcho for the men's rodeo, had combined their companies into the UPRC two years ago. At first, it had been exactly what the two organizations needed to stave off bankruptcy. But lately, things hadn't been going well. Shelby was convinced that Blevins was doing something shady, but she didn't have any proof. Her brother Nash was undercover to see if he could find any dirt that Shelby could use to get rid of Jackson, his poor spending habits, and even worse behavior.

"Come on, Nash," Dolly muttered under her breath as she scrolled through his latest slew of unimpressive posts. A cactus? "Give me something to work with here."

"Hey, Dolly! Got any tips for me to go viral?" a voice called out.

She looked up to see Taylor Keating approaching her. Taylor was another problem. He wasn't sure what he wanted to be, and that made him difficult to brand. He was an excellent bullfighter, one of the guys who made sure that after a bull rider got tossed, the bull got back into the pens without harming itself or anyone else. But every now and then, Taylor would get it into his head that he wanted to "make it big" and entered into the bull-riding events. He was okay, but nothing to get excited about.

"Sure thing," she said, refusing to let a little thing like lack of talent stand in the way of a bull rider's fame and fortune. "Try using a trending hashtag and tag the rodeo's account for some extra visibility." Not that he knew what was trending or would even remember to do this. She'd offer to do it for him, but she didn't have the time. She had to make Nash a superstar. Or at least a fan favorite, otherwise it was going to look suspicious that he was still on the roster when better bull riders than him weren't making the cut. "It's opening day, so you should get some traffic."

Taylor looked like a deer in headlights. "Right," he said, staring at his phone in confusion.

"Here," she said, taking pity on him. "Sit on the fence over there and look thoughtfully into the distance."

"Huh?"

"I don't know, look at that hot dog vendor and think about what you want to order."

Taylor hopped up on the fence and hooked a leg over the rail. His gaze caught on something over her shoulder and his face broke out in a sexy smile.

"Not bad," she said, taking the picture and posting it to the UPRC rodeo's main site. She tagged him and added a few of the hashtags he could use. She went over to the fence to show him what she did. "Just use these hashtags when you take pictures around the rodeo today."

"Will do."

She glanced behind her to see what he was grinning at. It was her oldest sister, Loretta. She was pulling a beach wagon with her paintings in it, probably going to set them up in her pavilion in the vendor area of the rodeo. Dolly resisted the urge to shove Taylor off the fence for looking at her sister like that.

"She could probably use some help setting up," she said instead. Taylor was a nice guy for all his indecision, and Loretta could use a little of that right now.

"I've got a few minutes," he said, jumping down and heading over to Loretta with a cocky swagger.

Dolly hoped she was doing the right thing by sending him over there. But then Loretta's face lit up and they started to talk animatedly to each other. Feeling like she had done her good deed for the day, Dolly went back to her problem child: Nash Weaver.

As she walked toward the arena, she studied Nash's social media posts. His pictures were decent—hell, some of them were downright breathtaking—but his captions left much to be desired. As she swiped over the posts that fans tagged him in, a deep furrow etched between her brows. Her eyes darted from one social media platform to another, taking in the dismal engagement numbers and the slew of negative comments that seemed to follow Nash's every move like a dark cloud.

"Damn it, Nash," she muttered under her breath, shaking her head. "Why'd you have to go and mess up last season so bad?" She could only hope that he had taken her advice and gone to Trent Campbell's bull-riding school at the Three Sisters Ranch in Last Stand, Texas, during the off-season. Because the new season started now. There was no more time to fool around.

She knew promoting him wouldn't be easy after the season he'd had, but the depth of animosity from the fans was more than she'd bargained for. Dolly had managed to turn around reputations before—it was part of her job, after all—but the stakes on this were higher than normal. It wasn't just about convincing people that Nash was worth watching, it was about making sure that Jackson Blevins kept him on the payroll so Nash could snoop around and see what dirt Blevins was dealing in.

But even if Blevins wasn't doing anything illegal, he didn't mind putting lives at risk if it meant more tickets sold. He had to know there was an ongoing problem with drug tampering and betting on the animals. One cowboy, Mick Mickelson, had lost his career due to an injury when Hitchcock Livestock tampered with their bulls and tried to get insider information to place bets on the outcome of the rodeo events. Another cowboy, Ronnie Sunderland, died last year from riding a bull that had been injected with a steroid-like substance. Both times, her baby sister LeAnn could have been on that bull.

"Hey, Dolly!" Finn Laker, the new hotshot bull rider, called out as he swung into the saddle. He was scheduled to carry out the American flag in the opening day ceremony today. He flashed her a grin that did nothing for her but the buckle bunnies went crazy-pants over. "Ready to make me famous?"

"Always, cowboy," she replied, her voice steady as she raised her camera and snapped a series of him and his pretty palomino horse. She didn't know Finn all that well, but she did know his daddy. Or she used to. Dolly hoped that she wouldn't run into Jefferson Laker, or if she did, he wouldn't remember her. Jefferson was an oil baron who went through wives like Dolly went through shoes. She had met him during a dark time in her life, and he had been kind. But she was deeply ashamed of herself for the choices that had led her to that point. It would be better for everyone around if she never saw Jefferson Laker again.

"Did you get my good side?" Finn asked.

"No," she said. "Because you're sitting on it."

"You know it." He winked at her before turning his attention to the gathering crowd.

Dolly rolled her eyes but couldn't help the smile that tugged at her lips. He was as charming as he was rich. She should have sent him Loretta's way, instead of Taylor.

Nah, she couldn't risk it. She didn't know what she would even say to Finn's father if she ever saw him again.

Five years ago, Dolly had been let go from her professional cheerleader squad. She couldn't pay her rent and her bills were piling up. Her parents had been on the road with LeAnn, going from rodeo to rodeo across the country. In hindsight, Dolly should have tracked them down. But she had been too stubbornly independent. One of the girls she had been sharing an apartment with had been a stripper. Dolly couldn't dance or she might have tried it.

Another of her roommates got her a job as an escort. Dolly hadn't realized that the escort service was really a high-class prostitution ring until she went for her final interview with them. Of course by that time, her car had been repossessed, her credit cards were maxed out and she was a few weeks away from being kicked out of her apartment for not paying rent.

But she had made it clear that she wouldn't do anything sexual with any of the clients. They got a date and a friend for the evening. That was it. If they didn't like it, they could choose another girl. Dolly had been lucky with the men who'd selected her. No one tried to force her into having sex. They'd asked. They'd begged. They'd even offered her a great deal of money. But Dolly hadn't wanted to cross that line.

Until Jefferson Laker made her an offer she couldn't refuse.

Jefferson had wanted someone to spend the week with him at a destination wedding he was going to be a guest at. He picked Dolly out of the escort service's catalog because he recognized her as having been a pro cheerleader for his favorite football team. He was willing to pay her one hundred thousand dollars for one week. The caveat? She had to sleep with him.

At first, Dolly had refused. But then she thought about it. One week. One week and she could pay off all her bills, leave the escort service and start fresh with a new career in a new city. She could go home. She could pretend that it had never happened, if she wanted.

Dolly had it all planned out. She would do what she had to do for a week and then she'd start her new business as a YouTuber doing high-end makeup tutorials and workshop-related affiliate products. She thought it would be no big deal.

She had been wrong.

Dolly had managed to pretend to herself that having sex for money was a good business decision right up until she started sobbing on the end of the bed in a luxurious five-star hotel suite.

Jefferson could have raped her. He could have thrown

her out and demanded a refund. He could have asked the escort service to send another girl. He hadn't done any of that. He gave her a whiskey and sat next to her until she stopped crying. Then he said that she didn't have to do anything she didn't want to do. But if she still wanted the job, she would need to pretend that they were a couple. His most recent ex-wife was going to be at the wedding events all week. She was a huge football fan and had left him for a quarterback from a rival team last year.

Dolly had rallied and slept on the couch for the week. In public, she played the part of a smitten girlfriend, hanging on Jefferson's arm and on every word he spoke. She wore a tiny bikini and bounced around with drinks in her hand. Jefferson had been so happy with her performance, that not only had he paid the fee, but he let her keep the jewelry he had bought her to show off.

"Keep 'em," he had said when she tried to give them back. "If you get in another bind, sell them instead of yourself."

She still had the diamonds. It was a reminder of what could have happened and why she would never let things get that bad again.

Of course, now she had an ex-FBI agent and Jefferson's son in her small circle of acquaintances. Dolly woke up in cold sweats at night, picturing the confrontation when one or both of them found out about her escort days. Nash always had such a pole up his ass—she could only picture him looking down on her. And for some stupid reason, she wanted him to like her. They had butted heads all last year, but there had been a simmering attraction that had been underneath it all. She liked bantering with him, enjoyed spending time with him, even if he was grumpy as a grizzly before his first cup of coffee.

Finn, on the other hand, would waste no time telling all the cowboys. If her past got out, in addition to dealing with the sly looks and innuendos, Dolly could lose her job at the rodeo. The UPRC had a morality clause in their employment contracts to show their commitment to family values. And she needed this job. Her Dallas apartment was expensive as hell. If her reputation took a hit, Dolly could be canceled on social media. She could lose her social media followers and clout. Her ad revenue on her personal accounts would tank. It would be a professional disaster that rivaled the one that made her go to Leisure Industries.

But the personal disaster was what truly terrified her. If her family knew that she had worked as an escort, they'd be so disappointed in her. And that was something Dolly couldn't bear to think about.

So if that meant that she would have to keep Finn Laker and Nash Weaver at arms' length, it was a small price to pay. Unfortunately, she and Nash would have to work closely together this season—at least until he performed better in the rankings. She could only hope it wouldn't take him too long…

Chapter Two

Nash Weaver

THIS WOULD BE so much easier if he could hold his badge up to the peephole and demand, "FBI. Open up." Instead, Nash Weaver knocked on the motel door again. "Victor Lance. I know you're in there. I just want to talk to you."

The curtain shifted and he had a brief glimpse of the UPRC's former veterinarian who had been arrested for doping up a bull that had killed a man last year.

"I've said all I'm going to say until the trial," Dr. Lance said through the door. "Tell Jackson Blevins to stop bothering me."

Jackpot.

Nash wasn't there on behalf of Jackson Blevins, but he had a feeling the co-CEO of the UPRC was the main reason that Dr. Lance claimed he had been working alone when he shot up Sverre, an undefeated bull, last year with a steroid-like substance. Lance claimed that he had done it so the large bet he had placed on Sverre keeping his winning streak would pay out.

That had been true, but Nash didn't think that was the

entire story. Nash had a theory that Lance had been acting on Blevins's orders and that Blevins was actively involved in trying to fix the rodeo events so he could bet on them and win more frequently. If Nash could prove that, Shelby could use that evidence to out Blevins from the co-CEO spot and maybe, just maybe, she could turn the rodeo around so that it was profitable.

"I just need a few moments of your time. I think we have a way to make things work out better for each of us."

Another peer through the mustard-yellow curtain. "I know who you are."

Nash doubted that. Lance may know him as a bull rider, but he didn't know he was investigating the rodeo.

"Blevins sent you to work me over. I told him and I'm telling you, I'm sticking to our agreement."

Nash had to take a chance. "I'm not Blevins's goon. Shelby Miller sent me. And I'm not here to beat you up. I'm here to see if you can help my boss with information that will put Blevins behind bars."

"And how will that help me?"

"Depends on what information you've got."

The ugly curtain swished closed. "Pound sand."

Yeah, that was pretty much what he expected. "I'm going to leave my card here." Nash jammed a plain white card with his burner phone's number on it into the doorjamb. "Let me know if you change your mind."

After climbing into his truck, Nash waited a moment to see if Lance would open the door. When he didn't, he pulled out of the motel parking lot and headed to the Killeen rodeo.

As he drove, he called his sister who answered on the first ring. "What did he say?" Shelby asked.

"It's what he didn't say. But he did confirm that Blevins has something on him to make him willing to be the fall guy."

"He admitted that?"

"Not in so many words, but he thought Blevins had sent me to beat the snot out of him to make sure he keeps to the agreement."

"What agreement?"

"Good question."

"Damn it. I thought he'd talk once things settled down in the media, especially with his trial date approaching."

"He still might. This was just our first salvo. I've given him something to think about."

"Fuck," Shelby snarled.

Nash could relate. Helplessness had him wringing the steering wheel like it was Blevins's neck.

"This is our last season if I can't get out of this partnership with Blevins. He's running the business into the ground and the way the contracts were written, I either have to buy him out at double his investment—which I don't have—or sell him my shares—which he's not interested in buying. We're going to go bankrupt and I'm going to lose everything. I'm sorry I got you into this," she said miserably.

"No. Don't be sorry. You did the right thing. I'm going to nail this guy. I'm almost there." Nash had leads and bits of information that were starting to link together. "Trust me. By the time I'm done with him, he'll be behind bars and out of your life."

"Yeah?"

It was the hope in her voice that almost killed him. "I just need more time."

"Where are you?"

"I'm heading to Killeen now."

Shelby swore. "You're cutting it close, aren't you?"

"I'll be there in time for the bull-riding event."

"Nash, I've got bad news," she said.

Oh no, what now?

"Blevins wants to cut the dead weight, so to speak. He's going to remove the five lowest-scoring bull riders from Laredo's roster."

Shit. He had been dead last all through the previous season.

"Can't you override him?"

"Not without raising suspicion."

"I need to be on the roster so I can be at the rodeo and look around."

"I know that. And you know that. Just try to stay on the bull."

"Yeah, yeah," he bitched. Like it was that easy. "I'll do my best."

"I'll call you tonight. Good luck."

He was going to need it. While a part of him would be relieved not to get on a bull again, the part of him that needed to be behind the scenes at the rodeo chafed at the ultimatum. Nash owed Shelby for everything she had sacrificed for him so that he could escape their nightmare of a home and live his dream as an FBI agent...until the shit hit the fan and his career tanked. He needed to catch Blevins because it was Nash's turn to be there for his sister.

Three years ago, Nash had been a rising star in the bureau, making a name for himself with a string of high-profile arrests and convictions. But it only took one asshole who thought he was above the law—and who was connected enough to get away with it—and suddenly, Nash found himself benched while they investigated his claims.

His partner, Special Agent Miles Garrett, had been regularly accessing classified databases for personal reasons. Instead of using this information for official investigations, he had been discreetly checking up on friends, family, and acquaintances.

"It's not a big deal," Miles had said. "Everyone does it."

Nash first noticed it during a routine cybersecurity training session. The bureau emphasized the importance of maintaining the integrity of classified databases, and agents were trained to use these resources judiciously for official investigations.

At first, he assumed Miles was working on a sanctioned project without him, and that was okay. But then it kept happening and Miles's actions went beyond what would be considered routine background checks for professional reasons.

Nash might have let it go, even though it killed him to look away. But then Miles acted on the information in two very different situations. The first was to help out Miles's sister-in-law who had been accused of being involved in a cybercrime ring. She was innocent. But that wasn't the point. Miles found a flaw in the evidence and tipped off her lawyer about the potential legal loophole and basically orchestrated a behind-the-scenes maneuver that led to the charges being dropped.

Nash reported that up the chain.

Miles got a slap on the wrist and Nash was told to let it drop. Justice had been served.

"No one was hurt by Miles's actions," his boss had said.

Things got very chilly between him and his partner after that. The whispers also started around that time. He would find packages of gummy rats in his desk and catnip mice in his car. Very funny. Very mature. You would think that government agents were beyond that sort of thing.

You'd be wrong.

And naturally, Miles didn't stop using bureau resources for personal use. The next time, Miles claimed he was helping out a childhood friend who was going through a nasty divorce. He gathered intelligence on the husband's financial dealings and potential misconduct. It was nothing the bureau was involved in, but from a quick look at the evidence, Nash could tell that the husband was using business funds for escorts. Needless to say, Miles's friend's lawyer had a field day with that one.

Nash reported that up the chain too.

This time Miles was suspended without pay while the bureau looked into his activities. Nash had taken no pleasure in doing it. He just wanted to do the right thing. Nothing official happened, but Nash's assignments soon started to revolve around sitting at his desk and doing busy work. Miles requested a transfer and received it.

The higher-ups didn't seem too eager to get Nash back

on the field or assign him a new partner. And then a friend had pulled him aside and advised him to take an early retirement. Otherwise, he was destined for every crap assignment coming down the pike. The term "whistleblower" was apparently synonymous with "traitor" in certain areas.

Enraged that he was the one being punished when all he did was report what he saw, Nash had been disillusioned enough to cash out and get his private investigator license. Business had been slow, so when Shelby had told him her concerns, he had the opportunity to help his sister out by posing as a bull rider and infiltrating the UPRC to see what dirt he could dig up on her partner.

There was only one problem—Nash absolutely sucked at bull riding. His hands were calloused from gripping bull ropes and his body was battered from countless spills in the dirt. And he didn't even want to go into the damage his pride had taken in the past year. The last time he had ridden a bull had been in college. His body had changed a lot since then. He also didn't remember the ground being as hard in those days.

"Nash," Shelby had begged him. "I need you. I've sunk every last dime I have into this merger and Jackson Blevins is just pissing it away."

"There's nothing illegal about that," Nash had said.

"Yeah, but I've been hearing rumors about deals he's made, and I'm afraid of him."

That was all it took. No one was allowed to scare his sister. Not after Shelby had been a mother to him when their own was in jail, and then stood toe-to-toe with her after she found religion and wanted back into their lives. Shelby had negotiated with her to sign off on Nash's early entrance to college—out of state and out of that toxic environment.

After a year of being on the rodeo circuit, Nash had finally found out enough to validate Shelby's fears. Blevins was doing deals without consulting her, taking risks that the board had not only never approved of, but had never discussed, and he was doing it like a man who didn't care if he was burning bridges. But there wasn't anything solid they could pin on Blevins yet that pointed to him doing anything illegal.

The key word was *yet.*

Nash studied all the employee records until he could call up details about their lives without a second thought. He'd been over and over the financial records and, using Shelby's passwords and passcodes, had gone over every inch of the Dallas headquarters.

Nada.

The latest scheme Blevins had come up with was to narrow down the farms and breeders who supplied the UPRC with stock animals down to three. Blevins had told the board it was to reduce their insurance liability and the extra cost of veterinarian services for all the drug testing the rodeo had been forced to do because of the accidents that had caused one death and one career-ending injury. But Nash wondered if there was another reason why the three stock contractors had been picked over all the other applicants.

The Viking Ranch of Charlo, Montana.

Jaripeo Ranch of Guanajuato, Mexico.

Rocky Ridge Ranch in Czar, Alberta.

That's where Nash was concentrating his investigation. But he needed to stay in the rodeo's good graces to do so.

Nash's gut said Blevins was corrupt and knee-deep in some serious shit. Unfortunately, Blevins wasn't an idiot. It was so much easier when the bad guys were dumb.

His phone rang and Nash flicked his eyes toward the mini-screen on his instrument panel.

PITA is what flashed up to identify the caller. This wasn't a bread vendor. In this case, it stood for pain in the...

"What do you want, Dolly?" he drawled.

"Where the hell are you?" a cute but irate voice snarled over the truck's speakers.

Dolly was the drop-dead gorgeous PR person for the rodeo. Shelby liked her and trusted her enough to let her know his true identity. Nash thought that had been a mistake. Dolly had a sketchy background, and her sister was engaged to Shane Calland, the owner of the Viking Ranch, which was one of the exclusive stock contractors to the UPRC.

At first, Nash thought Dolly might be working with Blevins. But she hated the son of a bitch almost as much as Shelby did. Her soon-to-be brother-in-law, though, was still on Nash's short list of Blevins's accomplices. It had been Shane's bull who Lance had doped up and there had to be a reason why Blevins had picked the Viking Ranch out of all the other stock suppliers. Shane's ranch wasn't the biggest or the best, so it could be because Shane was willing to look the other way. It wasn't a strong theory, but he was keeping it in the back of his mind until something better came alone.

"I'm on the highway," he said.

"You're supposed to be doing promo shots with me right now. It's opening day. We want to start this season out strong."

He allowed himself to picture her standing in the rodeo grounds. She'd be wearing tight jeans and a clingy T-shirt that would make him forget that he was supposed to be concentrating on his investigation and not on her curves and sweet smile.

"Must have slipped my mind," he said, adjusting himself. They had been bantering back and forth for over a year now and one of these days he was going to have to kiss her, just so he could stop thinking about it. But until he lost all semblance of control, he had to be satisfied with just bickering with her. It was almost as good as what he imagined kissing her would be like.

"The hell it did," she said.

Ever since last year, Dolly had been on his case to build up a following on social media because his abysmal scores in bull riding would have disqualified any other athlete from competing at as many UPRC events as he'd been attending. Turns out she might be able to tell him "I told you so," if he didn't turn it around today.

Nash had argued with her all last season, *"I didn't join this rodeo to take selfies. I've got a job to do. And it's not staying on a bull for eight seconds or taking stupid pictures— hashtag rodeo dreams."*

Nash's daily routine was a carefully choreographed dance of deception. Mornings were spent at the rodeo grounds or practicing his bull-riding skills and putting on a display of bravado with the other cowboys. He'd talk shop, share stories of broken bones and close calls, careful never to let the mask slip even for a moment. Lunch was usually spent huddled in the corner of some greasy spoon diner, chewing on a stale sandwich while listening for whispers about anything that might point him in a new direction.

"You'd better up your game," Dolly had said. *"Because if you don't start bringing something to the table, you'll be out on your denim-clad ass. You don't want to tip Blevins off that you're anything but a bull rider."*

One of the really annoying things about Dolly was she tended to be right on the money with these things. At first, he had been "the new guy," and no one said much, but after last season, Nash was starting to be accepted as one of "them." And cowboys forgot to be cautious when talking about shadier things. Nash already knew where a guy could go to spend some money to spend some time with a few working women in each rodeo city. That hadn't pointed back to Blevins, though.

Nash had seen contraband come over from some of the cowboys from other countries, too, but that didn't seem to tie back to the rodeo as much as it did to the individual cowboy who wanted to start an extracurricular business in the States. Nash wouldn't put it past Blevins to seek out a kickback or a finder's fee, but based on what Nash had seen, that wasn't happening either.

"Your last post was a picture of a cactus." Dolly sighed

in exasperation, bringing Nash back to their present conversation. "And that was two weeks ago."

"I've been concentrating on my bull riding." That was a flat-out exaggeration, but he didn't want her to know too much about his investigation, just in case she slipped up and said something to her brother-in-law. Her sister Reba, who was Shane's fiancée, knew his real identity too. So maybe that was why his investigation had stalled.

"Pictures or it didn't happen."

"I forgot."

"You forgot," she said flatly. "This is why I have to stick to you like glue."

He pushed a sexy image of her pressed up against him out of his mind.

"Fine." Nash knew there was no use arguing with her. Although, he couldn't shake the feeling that it was already too late to salvage things in the online popularity contest Dolly wanted to sign him up for. "I can free up some time after my ride today."

"You better," she warned and hung up.

Chapter Three

Nash Weaver

AFTER ARRIVING AT the Killeen Rodeo Grounds, Nash parked in the area reserved for the cowboys and reluctantly headed over to the bull pens. "Another day, another kick in the ass," he muttered under his breath, adjusting the brim of his cowboy hat. It was not just being stuck in backwater towns with nothing but rodeo hicks and cow shit for company. It was that he should have still been in the FBI working on important cases.

But this case was vital to Shelby's success, so he would pretend to be someone he wasn't. Even if that made him feel like their grifter father every time he sauntered into the rodeo. Nash put those feelings aside because he couldn't afford any missteps, any moments of vulnerability that might expose his true identity.

There was a price to pay for living a double life, though, and Nash felt it keenly. As he buckled up his chest protection and headed out to join the other riders, he realized he was lonely. Any shared camaraderie was false and he felt like a con artist being fake to good people who took him at face value.

The only person he could be himself with was Dolly and there was a small part of him that couldn't quite take her off his suspect list. He wondered, though, if that was just an excuse he was giving himself to keep her at arm's length.

And yet, despite the constant strain of keeping up appearances, Nash couldn't deny that there was something strangely intoxicating about the rodeo world—the raw energy of the crowd, the lure of danger and excitement. Being undercover was almost like being back in the field again.

"Hey there, Nash," a voice drawled from behind him. "You look about as excited to be here as a steer at a branding."

Nash turned to see Barney, one of the rodeo clowns he'd befriended over the past year and a half. "Just thinking about how I'm going to stay on Tornado," he said, forcing a half-smile.

"Guts will get you on the bull, but it's skill that keeps you there."

"Skill, huh?"

"Yup. And a little bit of crazy. Just grip him with your knees and keep your ass in the saddle," Barney replied, slapping Nash on the back.

Yeah, like it was that easy, Nash thought. But he kept that sentiment to himself, instead saying, "I can do that."

"Damn straight," Barney declared, adjusting his oversized suspenders. "Now, if you'll excuse me, I've got to make a few thousand people laugh."

"Knock 'em dead," Nash said, forcing a smile.

As he watched Barney strut off toward the arena, Nash felt a flicker of envy. The rodeo might be a far cry from the life he'd known as an FBI agent, but at least it was honest work. Barney was doing something he loved, something Nash desperately missed. He supposed if he was getting any traction on the investigation, he might have felt differently.

But for now, all he could do was watch and keep up appearances, waiting for the day when he could finally step out of the shadows and bring his sister Blevins's head on a proverbial platter. Until then, he'd have to hold on tight and ride it out like the rest of the cowboys, hoping against hope that he wouldn't get tossed on his ass.

Again.

"Hey, Weaver!" called out a voice, as Nash was heading into the chutes for his ride. He turned to see Finn Laker, the UPRC's newest all-star. "You're up next. Think you can handle Tornado?"

"Guess we'll find out soon enough."

If Finn was the golden child of the rodeo, Nash was on the opposite end of the spectrum. He had the worst record in the league and people were starting to grumble about Nash being at events while more qualified cowboys had been edged out. This was the first ride of the season and he needed to score high enough to stop the gossip and rumors. He had to stay with the UPRC, to unearth Blevins's secrets without revealing his own. The balance was precarious, like riding a bull—one wrong move and he'd be thrown.

Nash got into position while the rodeo hands steadied Tornado into the chute. The bull was a big, mean son-of-a-bitch, but that described most of the bulls. Settling on the bull's wide back, Nash adjusted his grip on the bull rope.

"Eight seconds. That's all you need," Finn said, as the gate swung open.

Nash needed to do this. For Shelby.

The gate burst open, and Tornado exploded into the ring. With a surge of adrenaline and determination, Nash held on tight as Tornado bucked and twisted, trying to shake him loose. The roar of the crowd and the pounding of hooves filled his ears, drowning out the doubts and fears that plagued him. For those brief moments, he was a bull rider—nothing more, nothing less. Nash's world narrowed to the violent jerks and twists beneath him. Muscle and sinew strained against the fury of the bull, his focus laser-sharp on maintaining his precarious grip. Eight seconds stretched into an eternity until finally, the buzzer sounded, and Nash was flung from Tornado's back like a rag doll tossed by an angry child.

The sweetest sound he had ever heard was that eight-second buzzer. He had managed to stay on the damned thing. Maybe those lessons with Trent over the winter break had paid off after all. He dismounted and stumbled away from the heaving beast who was panting from the exertion. Nash could relate. He ignored his own shaky legs while he returned to the back area where the VIP fans were allowed. All he wanted was a shower and a beer, though.

"Nash," Dolly called out as she moved through the crowd with an infectious energy that made people stop and stare. She was like a magnet, pulling people toward her with her contagious laughter and genuine charm. He watched her with fascination, admiring the way the sunlight danced in her blond hair. She was the sexiest thing he had ever seen. Too bad she was such a pain in his ass.

"Damn, that girl's got a laugh that could bring a man to his knees," Finn said from beside Nash when Dolly stopped to talk with a group of barrel racers.

Dolly wasn't just a pretty face, though. Beneath her confident exterior lay a sharp mind that put her expertise in social media to good use for the UPRC rodeo. More than once, Nash had found himself impressed by her resourcefulness and grit.

"And a tongue sharper than a knife," Nash said. And she wasn't afraid to use it either.

"Y'know, I heard she used to be a professional cheerleader," Finn continued, taking a swig of his beer. "Hard to believe she traded the big-city lights for this dusty old rodeo."

"She must have had her reasons," Nash said.

"Probably aged out," Finn said. "But damn, I'd hit that."

Nash wanted to hit him, but he tamped it down. He didn't have any reason to feel protective toward Dolly. He just didn't like Finn disrespecting her. But he also wasn't in the mood for a lecture about his social media presence or lack of it, so he moved through the crowd quickly. He wasn't exactly running away from her—more like walking fast.

"Hey, y'all!" a voice called out from the sidelines, drawing his attention. It was Lila, one of the girls who followed the rodeo all over the country. She held out a bucket of ice with a bunch of beer bottles sticking out. "Thought you might need some refreshments."

"Let's get some of that," Finn said to him with an elbow in his ribs.

"A beer sounds pretty good," Nash said, even though out of the corner of his eye he could see that Dolly was still trying to get to him.

"That's not all you can get," Finn said as they walked over to Lila.

Nash was aware that Lila would gladly go home with either one of them, or both, if the rumors were true. But he didn't have time for a romp in the sheets, even if he had been interested in Lila's no-strings offer.

He took the ice-cold bottle with a grateful nod. Yet he still searched out where Dolly was. He had promised to do a few promotional photos for her. If he put it off, it would only make her more determined to hunt him down. Another bull rider, Keith Kilgore, had stopped her and was obviously trying to get her to take a picture of him.

Better Keith than him.

Still, Nash didn't like the way the guy was aggressively squaring off against Dolly. He wondered if he should step in, but then she said something, and Kilgore backpedaled a few feet before turning tail and running.

Thatta girl.

"Cheers, boys," Lila said, raising her own bottle in salute.

"Cheers." Nash clinked bottles with her and tried not to see the offer in her eyes.

He scanned the VIP area instead, trying not to stare too closely at what looked to be a drug deal or an exchange of some illicit goods happening. He didn't recognize the one doing the selling, but the buyer was Taylor Keating, Barney's son. Nash sidled a step in that direction to get a better vantage point, but Lila stopped him with a hand on his arm.

Damn it. He hated that this cowboy gig got in the way of him doing his job.

"You did real good today, Nash," she said, batting her eyelashes at him.

"Didn't beat my time," Finn said with a frown. And even though Nash had stayed on his bull for eight seconds, his score wasn't good enough for a second ride.

"Nobody can touch your time," Nash said, taking a step back so Finn could lean on the railing closer to Lila.

Lila giggled when Finn reached into the ice bucket and slipped a cube down her shirt.

Dolly would have socked him one if he tried that shit with her. When he glanced back at where he saw the exchange happening, both parties had faded back into the ground. Crap! Nash made it a point to find out what Taylor had been buying and who the cowboy was who was selling. He hoped for Barney's sake that it was not what it had looked like. But if it was, he hoped from the investigation standpoint that the seller had ties to Blevins.

Nash's phone buzzed. He saw it was a text from Shelby. *I'm sorry. I tried to stop this. But I can't. You're off the roster for tomorrow and Laredo.*

"Son of a bitch," he snarled.

Lila flinched back and Finn raised his eyebrows.

"Sorry," Nash said, wiping a hand down his face. "Bad

news. I've got to go."

He had to get out of here. Ducking into the locker room, Nash grabbed his gear and went out the back. All he wanted to do was get into his truck and head back to his motel. He would have to find a way to investigate Blevins without being part of the rodeo. It pissed him off because he felt like he was failing Shelby again.

Shelby was calling him now. Reluctantly, he answered it as he was heading toward the parking lot.

"What now?" he asked.

"Dolly seemed to have a good idea about you appealing to the fans more by doing promos around the rodeo."

"Seriously? Why does that even fucking matter anymore?" He pinched the bridge of his nose with his fingers. He didn't mean to take this out on Shelby, but he was so frustrated with the situation.

"Look, it'll give you a reason to be on-site. I'll text her to have a guest pass for you at the gates."

"A guest pass?"

"It's the best I can do. Maybe Dolly has some other ideas."

Of that, he didn't have a doubt. She always had ideas. The problem was they tended to skate the line of rule breaking and lying. Still, he couldn't deny she got results. He wondered though if that made her more like Miles and his father. The comparison didn't sit well with him. But the thought that maybe he'd judged Miles too harshly niggled at the back of his mind. Did the ends justify the means or was that the slippery road that had led his father down his life of crime?

"Meet her by the barrel-racing events. She'll fix this. It's what she does."

Nash stopped dead in his tracks. He wanted to get the hell out of here. He didn't like the feeling of being forced out of a situation again. But he didn't have a choice. Not if he wanted to help nail Blevins to the wall.

Chapter Four

Dolly

DOLLY WASN'T SURE if it was anger that was buzzing through her right now or anticipation. Sure, she was pissed that Blevins had thrown a wrench into Nash's investigation. But she was also glad that this gave her a chance to show Shelby that she was up for the challenge of making her brother a viral sensation.

Even if it was against his will.

After the whole fiasco with Jefferson Laker and the escort service, Dolly had tried to build safeguards into her life so that she'd never be that desperate for a job again. She was the queen of side hustles, from monetizing her YouTube and TikTok accounts, to putting up T-shirt designs on Etsy. At least she had had the good sense to put some of Jefferson's money into her education. Her marketing degree had only got her so far in public relations. The rest had been self-taught through tutorials and mentorships and plain old trial and error.

There had been a lot of error.

Unfortunately, that had fed into her workaholic lifestyle and when she got this job at the UPRC when it merged, Dolly thought maybe—just maybe—she could let herself take it easy. But not right away. First she had to prove to the UPRC that she was invaluable—that would give her job security. And then Jackson Blevins decided to mess with that. She had to get butts in the seats. Trying to get posts to go viral was exhausting.

Damn Blevins to all hell.

She saw Nash striding toward her and the anger pouring off him would be Instagram gold with all that smolder. Dolly resisted the urge to fan herself. Maybe it had been watching him go eight seconds on that bull that made her toes curl in her boots—and she wasn't a horny buckle bunny. She had a slight fear that Nash could bring out her inner floozy if he just smiled at her more.

The Texas heat hadn't even reached the high nineties today, so she couldn't blame that on why she was so hot and bothered. Her fingers itched to film him, but she wanted to give him some privacy while he dealt with the emotions of being fired by the man he was investigating.

She spoke first when he came up to her. "Don't let Blevins get to you. He must have taken his asshole pills today. I've been dodging his calls all morning so he's been texting me suggestions on how to make the UPRC go viral. And some of the shit has been pretty questionable."

Nash's glower grew even grimmer under the brim of his Stetson. "Questionable how?"

She checked her texts. "Wet T-shirt contests."

"That's a sexual harassment lawsuit waiting to happen."

"I reminded him that we needed to bring in families, not horn dogs."

"What did he say?"

"His next suggestion was an after-hours club."

"What did you say?"

"That I would look into it, but I thought that the arena fees wouldn't cover what we could charge for admission."

"Why is he bothering you with this?"

"He likes to text me." Dolly shuddered. Blevins gave her the creeps. She made sure she was never alone with him. He pushed all her warning buttons whenever he looked at her. "Anyway, I'm sorry you got cut."

"I don't get it. I finally went eight seconds today." Nash moved up to walk next to her. She hated that the innocent brush of his arm against hers threw her off her game.

"Yeah, and we need to make the most of it on social media. If we can build the excitement, Blevins might put you back on the roster for Laredo."

"You think?"

No, she didn't. But she smiled anyway, as if she did. "But just in case, we're going to do a deep dive on you to see what we can get traction on. So you're mine, cowboy, for the next hour." Dolly realized how that sounded and did her best to cover up her embarrassment. "I've got footage of your ride, but we're going to do a lot of candid shots all around Killeen today to fill out your content."

Nash grunted sourly.

Her attraction to Nash was becoming increasingly difficult to ignore. It had slowly built between them all last year when all the sniping and snarling at each other turned to a weird type of flirtation. Weird because he wanted to keep things professional and she didn't want him to look too closely at her past, and yet both of them found reasons to be together. There was something magnetic about his tall, dark-haired figure, even when he was grumpy and introverted. But his pissy attitude grated on her nerves something fierce.

Luckily, Nash was too annoyed to catch what could have been taken as a double entendre.

"It's bad enough I've got to pretend to be a cowboy in real life. Now I've got to make up a fake persona online as well? Are you sure this is going to help? Sounds like a waste of time to me. And I don't have a lot of time to waste—especially if my time at the rodeos will be limited."

"You need to get some fans buzzing about you on our pages. If you get enough interest, Shelby can make a play for you sticking around on the PR side."

Around them, the rodeo thrummed with life. Children shrieked with delight, while the scent of sizzling barbecue mingled with the earthy tang of livestock. Cowboys milled about, their spurs chiming like an erratic melody against the thumping bass of country rock blaring from speakers. The smell of manure and hay mixed with the scents of barbecue and popcorn from nearby food trucks.

Nash's jaw clenched, his gaze lingering on a distant pen where a bronco kicked up a fierce protest. "I think it might be too late for all that."

"It's never too late," Dolly said, forcing herself to be sunshiny and upbeat when truly all she wanted to do was take him by the ear and drag him over to the hay bales.

Nash sagged in defeat. "Fine. What do you suggest we

do?"

"First, let's get some pictures of you looking like a rodeo star."

"I'm not a rodeo star," he said, exasperated.

She held up a hand. "We're pretending."

"This is stupid," he muttered.

"Here, stand next to this pen and look cool." Dolly watched as Nash reluctantly posed.

"Look," he said. "I don't mean to give you a hard time. I'm sorry."

"It's okay. I get it. I've been fired too. A few times. It's something that doesn't get better the more you experience it."

"I guess not," he said and gave her a smile that made her heart flutter.

"Yeah, just like that," she said softly. She took a few photos from different angles. "Okay come on, let's find more backgrounds."

As they walked, Dolly glanced around and when they were alone she thought it was safe enough to talk about her theories about Blevins.

"So he's got to be involved with either illegal gambling or doping, right?" Dolly said.

"I wouldn't put it past him. Hickory Livestock was betting on the bulls that Blevins supplied the women's rodeo before the companies merged. I don't see him letting an opportunity for profit to go by. But he claims he didn't know Hickory was betting on the outcome."

"Shelby didn't know," Dolly pointed out.

"My sister likes to see the good in people."

"And you don't?"

"Sweetheart, I know better."

It gave her the shivers when he called her that, even if she knew he didn't mean anything by it. When he first came to the rodeo, she thought he was just some shady cowboy. But then he stood by her sister Reba and believed that she had been innocent last year when some bulls tested positive for enhancement drugs. Reba was one of the veterinarians that the UPRC kept on staff.

When Shelby had trusted Reba and Dolly with the knowledge that her brother was undercover, Dolly decided to cut Nash some slack. But not that much slack. She still had a job to do. "Do you miss being a Fed?"

"No comment," he said.

"Oooh, touched a nerve, did I?" But he didn't look like he was in the mood for teasing. "Sorry," she said. "I didn't mean to pry. Just trying to get to know you."

"Why?"

"It makes my job easier." And she was borderline obsessed with him. It wasn't pretty, but she found herself taking more pictures than necessary of him. She wanted to get to know him better, but she had been holding herself back because if he decided to investigate her, he'd come up with an eyeful. And she didn't want him to know about the poor choices she had made. Not until she was sure he wouldn't judge her for them.

"Yeah, but you're not trying to promote me: Nash Weaver, former Fed. You're trying to make Nash Weaver, shitty bull rider, go viral. All you have to do is lie."

The way he said lie—like it was "murder" or "kick a

kitten"—made her uncomfortable. "It's not lying to create a good story."

"Yes, it is."

It took everything she had not to come back with, "No, it isn't." Because she could seriously see them taunting each other like a couple of toddlers. She decided to change the subject. "What have you got on Blevins?"

"Nothing actionable." He shifted his weight and glanced around the rodeo grounds, eyes narrowing. "But he's got something on Victor Lance that's making him clam up and take the blame for doping up Sverre last season."

"Vanessa is going to push for manslaughter," Dolly said. Vanessa Sunderland was Ronnie's widow. "It was hard enough to get her to lay off putting Sverre down." Sverre was her brother-in-law's bull. Shane agreed to put him out to pasture, and once the bull had a year of clean health, he was planning on selling him out to stud.

"Maybe when it gets more real for him, Lance will cut a deal."

"What if he doesn't?" she asked.

"Then I'll catch Blevins on something else. I have a feeling that there's something suspicious about the stock contractors he's hand selected."

"Well, you can cross Shane Calland and the Viking Ranch off your list," she said, trying not to let her anger show.

"Ooh touched a nerve, did I?" Nash used her own words against her.

She just wanted to smack him sometimes. "They have

nothing to do with whatever illegal shit Blevins is up to."

"Why? Because your sister Reba is going to marry Shane?"

"Yes," she said honestly. "You know from all the nonsense that went on last year that Shane wouldn't do anything to harm his bulls. And Reba hates Blevins after that 'Killer on a Killer' event he wanted to do, showcasing LeAnn riding Sverre." Their sister LeAnn's nickname was Killer Keller and Sverre had just killed Ronnie Sunderland. Blevins's bright idea had been to capitalize on that. That was when Dolly became invested in taking the son of a bitch down.

"I haven't crossed anyone off the list yet."

The urge to shove him into a nearby pile of horseshit was almost overwhelming. But then she realized it was better if she just tormented him with social media.

"Keep posing and smiling for these pictures. Can you undo a few buttons on your shirt? And maybe take that stick out of your ass?" She pretended not to notice the irritated glare he shot her way.

"Dolly, come here," she heard her sister Reba call out to her.

The midday sun beat down on the rodeo grounds, casting long shadows behind the barns and animal pens. Dolly shielded her eyes with a hand, scanning the area until she spotted Reba.

"I'm a little busy."

"Don't put your sister off on my account," Nash said. "We can be done here."

"Not yet we're not," she said. "Let's go see what she

wants."

"Why do I have to go?"

"I don't know. Maybe there'll be a clue as to what Blevins is up to over there?"

"Or maybe you'll find something else for me to take a picture of with," Nash said.

He wasn't wrong.

But at least he followed her over to where her sister was kneeling.

"Please tell me you're not elbow-deep in a cow's vagina? Because I'll barf," Dolly said, ignoring Nash's amused look.

"Look at this little guy," Reba said. "He's a *heilan coo*."

"Don't you mean cow?"

"Same thing."

Dolly looked where she was pointing. A baby Highland cow stood on stocky little legs in the middle of the pen. It had a fluffy reddish-brown coat and its shaggy hair hung into its large, expressive eyes. It had a button nose, and short, tufted ears. There were two small, curved horns on either side of its head. It bleated at them, a sweet little cry.

"What on earth is that doing here?" Dolly took several pictures.

"That's Donnan," Reba said. "His name means little brown one."

Nash folded his arms, his gaze flicking between Dolly and the calf. "Where did he come from?"

"Originally Scotland," Reba said, standing up and dusting off her knees.

"I know that this is a rodeo and all," Nash said. "But the crowd isn't going to stand for anyone roping him."

"Of course not." Reba scowled. "Blevins wanted us to have a traveling petting zoo. He arranged for this little one to be our star attraction."

"Blevins set this up?" Nash's interest perked up.

Dolly moved closer to the sign attached to the temporary fencing. Rocky Ridge Ranch was one of the three stock contractors that Blevins set up to exclusively supply stock to the rodeo. "You know, Nash, Donnan could be a great promotional tool for you."

"Really?" he asked skeptically, glancing toward the calf again as if reevaluating its potential.

"Absolutely. People love cute animals. Think of the attention you'd get."

Nash frowned, his jaw muscles working as he chewed on the idea. Clearly, he wasn't thrilled about wasting time on photo shoots or petting zoos when there was investigating to be done.

"Lighten up, Nash. He could be good for your image," Dolly insisted. "Imagine the likes we'd get with you and Donnan together."

"Likes don't lead to convictions," he muttered, yet his stance relaxed slightly as if considering the possibility.

She leaned in closer to him. "Take a look at the name of the stock contractor on the pen," Dolly whispered in his ear. "The more time you spend with this calf, the more we can dig into this contractor. You can't possibly believe that Jackson 'Wet T-shirt Contest and After-Hours Club' Blevins decided out of the blue that a petting zoo is the way to get more money."

"You have a point."

"And we'll be able to cross Shane's ranch off your list."

He turned to her, their noses almost touching. She should step back. But she couldn't bring herself to. A frisson of awareness tingled over her skin. Her lips were inches from his. Was this it? Would they finally kiss? Her gaze flicked to his lips and back again.

"We?" he said.

Nope. He looked annoyed with her, not overcome with lust. Damn it.

"You're going to need me as a cover, taking pictures." She took a step away from him and tried not to meet Reba's assessing look. "Otherwise, people will wonder why you're snooping around the Rocky Ridge Ranch pens."

Nash hesitated for a moment before sighing in resignation. "Fine, let's do it," he said, his voice laced with annoyance. Dolly felt a flicker of satisfaction at having won him over.

"Mind if I take a few pictures of Donnan with Nash?" she asked her sister.

"Be my guest—just watch where you step."

"What other animals are you going to have in the petting zoo?" Nash asked as they climbed into the pen.

Reba shrugged. "The usual. I've got a miniature horse, some rabbits, baby chicks and goats. Why?"

"Just gathering information. I wonder why Shelby didn't mention it to me."

"She might not have known," Dolly said. "In my experience, Blevins doesn't share a lot of information with her."

"That's part of the problem."

Reba was called away on some veterinarian business,

which left them alone with Donnan.

"Isn't he just the cutest thing you've ever seen?" Dolly gushed, reaching out to stroke the soft fur on Donnan's head. The calf nuzzled against her hand, clearly enjoying the attention.

Nash simply grunted in response, his arms crossed over his chest as he observed the scene with a mix of amusement and annoyance. "Why a petting zoo?" he muttered, eyeing Donnan warily.

"Maybe he's smuggling things in their pens?"

"It's worth a look." Nash sighed, uncrossing his arms and crouching down to get a closer look at Donnan. The calf eyed him curiously, sniffing at his outstretched hand before allowing Nash to pet him. "He's cute—I'll give you that."

"Right? Now let's take some photos and videos for your social media." Dolly pulled out her phone and started snapping pictures, capturing candid shots of Nash and Donnan interacting. "We want the fans to link you and Donnan together. He's charming—you're not."

"Thanks," Nash said dryly.

"But you can talk and interact with the fans and Donnan can't. That makes you valuable to have around."

Despite his earlier reluctance, Nash smiled as the calf playfully licked his hand.

"See? This isn't so bad," Dolly teased, her own grin widening as he continued to pose with the calf. "A little smiling wouldn't hurt."

"Smiling isn't my style."

"Try it on for size." She circled them, capturing the

moment. "It'll be good for your image."

"I thought all girls wanted a bad boy."

"Bad boy, yes. Grumpy boy, no."

His lips twitched, a reluctant smile forming.

"See? Not so hard." Dolly clicked away. The contrast between the gruff man and the gentle creature was panty-melting and ovary-exploding.

"Are we done yet?"

"Not just yet." She continued filming as Nash's guard dropped, revealing a hint of warmth in his interactions with the calf. "I don't suppose you'd be willing to take your shirt off."

"Fuck off," he said good-naturedly.

It had been worth a shot.

But they were attracting attention. A few other bull riders in the area took notice. They sauntered over, smirking at the sight before them.

"Hey, Weaver!" one of them called out, chuckling as he leaned against the fence. "Looks like you found a bull more your speed, huh?"

"It might even let you ride him without bucking you off," another added with a snort, causing the group to erupt into laughter.

"Back off, guys," Dolly snapped. "Nash is trying something new for his fans. There's nothing wrong with that."

"Fans?" the first rider scoffed. "That'll be the day."

"Fuck off," Nash said, not so good-naturedly this time.

The two snickered but moved along, leaving Nash fuming and Dolly glaring daggers at their retreating backs.

"Sorry about that." Dolly gave Nash an apologetic smile. "I didn't mean to make things worse."

"It's fine," Nash grumbled. "I'm used to it. Anyway, I'm getting hungry. You want to grab some lunch?"

"Really?" Dolly blinked, surprised by his sudden invitation, but pleased nonetheless. She hesitated, not wanting to get too personal with him. But then she reminded herself that getting to know him better could only help her market him, so Blevins never suspected he was being investigated. But she also had work to do and couldn't really get away right now.

"Yeah, it's the least I can do for taking my bad mood out on you before. I know you're just trying to help and I appreciate it."

"Thanks," she said. "That means a lot. Unfortunately, I need to take more shots of the other athletes and then I've got to get back to the mobile office and do some editing and update the UPRC's social media sites." Was she imagining the quick disappointment that crossed his face? "But how about dinner after the rodeo closes?"

"I'd like that," he said.

He would? Dolly tried not to read too much into that.

"Great," she babbled. "Give me a call and tell me where to meet you."

Nodding, Nash gave Donnan a pat on his cute little head and then gracefully climbed out of the pen and walked toward the food vendors. Dolly watched him go until Donnan nudged her hand with his head. She absently pet him.

"Well, do you think we can go viral?" she asked the calf.

Donnan didn't answer, but Dolly thought he'd give it his best shot.

Chapter Five

Dolly

THE BARBECUE RESTAURANT Nash chose was a down-home Texas joint, complete with the smell of mesquite smoke and bright neon beer signs flickering on the walls. Rodeo people filled the booths and barstools, laughing loudly over their brisket and ribs, their conversations a low hum of rivalry and camaraderie.

Dolly slid into a booth across from Nash and wasted no time checking the UPRC's Instagram page. She hadn't had time to edit the Donnan pictures, but the eight-second ride Nash had today was front and center. Nash's lean silhouette, swathed in shadows against the blinding midday sun, stood stark and arresting. The image captured him mid-ride, the bull beneath him a blurred fury of muscle and wild energy. He was a portrait of determination amid chaos. It was a good start.

"Got quite the eye, don't you?" Nash's voice cut through Dolly's concentration as she reviewed the reaction to her latest post.

"Comes with the territory," she murmured, her thumb hovering over the screen, tracking the influx of heart reactions and comments.

"That's some fancy editing. Makes me look almost competent."

"You did all right today. Blevins jumped the gun."

"Smoke and mirrors. And smoke doesn't last long. Let's hope your smoke holds out until we find something solid on Blevins." Nash reached for a bottle of barbecue sauce, turning it over in his hands. The label was faded, the edges peeling.

"Has the news trickled down to the other riders yet?" Dolly asked.

"Yeah, from what I hear Blevins fired four other bull riders."

"At least you weren't the only one," Dolly said, scrolling through her phone. "I've been looking at some strategies to engage fans and increase your visibility. We could create a series of videos featuring you and Donnan. You know, show off the softer side of a tough cowboy."

Nash scoffed, shaking hot sauce on the basket of fried pickles that the waitress had placed on the table. "And how's that going to help me become popular?"

"Fans want to feel like they know you. Your failures and successes become personal to them. Trust me, it'll help people connect with you more," Dolly insisted. "We could even host a live Q&A session with UPRC fans. Answer their questions, and then give them a glimpse into your life. I've got a detailed social media plan all worked out for you."

They ordered the special and it came out fast. Dolly snapped a picture of the generous spread before them: fall-off-the-bone ribs, tender brisket, and all the fixings, including coleslaw, baked beans, and corn bread.

"Really?" Nash asked as he caught her taking the photo, a teasing smile playing on his lips. "You're one of those people who has to document every meal?"

"Hey, it's for work."

"I guess I can let it slide this time."

Their knees brushed against the table. Their eyes met and her mouth went dry.

"You look pretty tonight," he said after several charged seconds.

"Thanks." Dolly was trying to remember how to breathe steadily.

Nash toyed with the saltshaker, while the conversations of the rodeo folks continued around them. Dolly was usually much better at making small talk, but sitting so close to Nash was short-circuiting her brain. "So tell me about yourself." That was lame, but at least it was something to break the tension.

"Not much to tell. I grew up in Georgia. I did some rodeo during college. Obviously, I didn't continue. How about you? Were you a high school cheerleader?"

Dolly nodded. "And junior high, and college and then I went pro."

"Why did you stop?"

"It wasn't my choice. I got too old." Dolly pushed aside those feelings. She stuffed a big piece of corn bread in her mouth to compensate.

"That sucks. I was forced out of my job too."

That was news. She quickly chewed and swallowed,

washing it down with a gulp of sweet tea. "What happened?"

Nash shook his head. "A long story and I don't want to get into it now."

She could understand keeping secrets, so she let it pass. "Were your parents disappointed when you left? My father couldn't care less, but my mother acted like someone died. Mom was a pageant queen, and she had wanted all her daughters to follow in her footsteps." Dolly fiddled with the frayed edge of the red-and-white checkered tablecloth. "Loretta gave it a go, but lost interest right away. She wanted to be an artist. Reba balked from the get-go. She'd have rather been in the barn than in a makeup chair. I did all right, but I never won a title. LeAnn gave her that, but then turned in her tiara for cowboy boots."

"Was she disappointed?"

"LeAnn? No, I think she was relieved to have the pressure off her. I know I was when I aged out of the pageantry scene. My mother, though? She was devastated."

"She must have been happy when the NFL picked you up."

Dolly hid a wince. "Thrilled. She taped every game I was in. If you're ever interested in being bored witless, let me know and I'll see if I can pry them out of her grip. What about your parents?" she asked, nudging again.

Nash took a big draw from his beer. "My father is a con artist, always looking for the next big score. I haven't heard from him in years."

Dolly winced. "Sorry to bring it up."

Nash shrugged. "It is what it is. My mother was the

same until she found religion. Now she's just the opposite—a devout woman who tries to save everyone's soul, including mine. She's a stickler for rules now. To her, everything is black and white, no room for gray areas."

"Sounds familiar," Dolly said.

"Who me?"

"Yeah you. You never go over the speed limit. You go out of your way to make sure your equipment is regulation."

"That's called following the rules. The rules are there for a reason."

Dolly shook her head. "No one cares if you bend them a little."

"I care," he said forcefully.

"I can see where you get your strong sense of duty from."

"More like my strong sense of guilt," he muttered under his breath.

"Is that why you went into the…" she looked around and lowered her voice to a whisper "…the bureau?"

"Let's just say it made me value the importance of abiding by the rules, and being honest whenever I can," he said, his tone tinged with bitterness.

She lowered her voice to a near whisper. "Being undercover must be hard for you then. It's a kind of lying, isn't it?"

He looked up at her sharply, as if he was surprised that she came up with that. "Yeah, exactly. I know it's a necessary part of the job, but it makes me feel like my dad."

"Well, you're doing this for good. I bet he did it for the

money."

"Some of the time. Most of the time, though, he did it because he could." Nash shook his head in disgust. "I can't tolerate anyone who lies. Myself included."

His words sent a shiver down Dolly's spine. All the more reason to keep him at arm's length.

She looked up to find Nash studying her, his dark eyes filled with curiosity.

"So you used to be a professional cheerleader," he said, as if trying to picture her in that role. "What was that like?"

Dolly felt a twinge of fear, wondering if he would somehow connect the dots to her past as an escort. She had been very careful to separate herself from Leisure Industries. There wasn't a digital trace to prove that she had ever been connected with the escort service. And yet, she knew she needed to grab his attention so he wouldn't probe any deeper. "You won't believe the crazy stunts we used to pull. It was like being in a reality show, but with more glitter."

Nash leaned in, intrigued. "Go on."

Dolly didn't like the shift back to her past, but she was glad to keep him talking. "All right, so picture this—it's Monday Night Football, and we're in the middle of this intense routine. We're doing these precision kicks, right? And just as I go for a high kick, I accidentally kick off my own shoe, and it goes soaring into the stands, hitting a hotdog vendor right in the ketchup bottle."

A wide grin spread across Nash's face. Dolly faltered. He was really good-looking when he did that. She wished she could get him to lighten up like that more often. When he smiled, it really did transform him into someone more approachable. She cleared her throat. "I had to finish the routine with one shoe on. My teammates called me Cinderella from then on."

"Did you ever find your prince?"

"Sadly no." She smiled as another memory came to her. Dolly was caught between mortification and hilarity.

"What's that look for?"

"I haven't thought about this one in a long time. I must have tamped it down in my memory. We had this grand plan for a surprise entrance during a championship game. I was supposed to descend from the rafters on a harness, landing gracefully on the field. Well, let's just say gravity had other plans. The harness got stuck, and I ended up swinging back and forth like a human pendulum. It was like a cheerleader version of Tarzan gone wrong. Our sound guy was quick on his feet. He queued up, "Yakety Sax"—you know the theme song from the old Benny Hill show? The crowd went wild."

"Were you scared?" he said.

She paused. He was supposed to have laughed—everyone else did when she told that story. Instead, he looked concerned. "Petrified," she said after a beat. But then because looking into his eyes was too intense, she concentrated on her food. "They eventually got me down and I cheered the rest of the game. We won. Thirty-three to twenty-five."

"That was very brave."

"Nah," she said, trying not to feel his words in her heart. "Brave is getting back on an enraged bull after not being on one in several years."

"Bet you looked better doing your thing than I did," he said.

"That's why they paid me the big bucks."

As the conversation lulled, Dolly tried not to stare at him like a lovesick buckle bunny. There was just something about him that did it for her. He looked rugged and handsome with his strong jawline and dark hair. Dolly's gaze lingered on the way Nash filled out a T-shirt. Why did he have to be so damned good-looking? What would it be like to kiss him?

The air between them felt charged, electric, but it was the underlying current of unease that Dolly noticed more than anything. He hated liars. Finding out she had been an escort would be a total deal-breaker, and potentially a heartbreaker, for her. She needed to keep this professional. Dolly focused on the clink of silverware and the murmur of voices at nearby tables, trying to ignore the growing tension.

"Did you hear about those Mexican fighting bulls they're bringing in for the next rodeo in Laredo?" a man at a neighboring table said.

"Sure did," another replied. "They say those bulls are meaner than a rattlesnake with a toothache. Can't wait to see how the riders handle 'em. This is the first time the UPRC has brought them in."

Dolly's eyes widened as she leaned in toward Nash, her voice barely above a whisper. "Do you think that's a clue?"

"At this point, I think anything could be a clue," he drawled.

"So are we going to investigate?"

"We?"

"Have camera will travel." She waggled her phone at him.

"I suppose it's as good of a cover as any. Can Reba get us close to the new bulls?"

"Sure. She's probably going to be doing drug testing on them. You're not thinking of trying to ride one of them, are you?"

"Why wouldn't I?" Nash replied, his eyebrow cocked defiantly.

"Because those bulls are crazy mean," Dolly said.

Nash's expression hardened, his jaw clenched. "Don't you think I can handle it?"

Well, to be honest…no. But she wasn't sure how to say that.

"You'd have a hard time getting access to them since you won't be on the roster," she said, hedging her answer.

"But if I can ride one for a reel of yours that could get some *buzz*." He flashed finger quotes at her.

Oh for Pete's sake, he sounded just like her sister LeAnn. Were all bull riders this crazy? "You just stayed on for eight seconds today for the first time in forever. Build on that."

"I plan on it."

They glared at each other over the table.

"I just don't want to see you get hurt," she said.

"I'm not going to get hurt," Nash snapped, his eyes narrowing. "Besides, it'll make a good TikTok, right?"

"Fine. Do whatever you want." Stubborn ass. It would serve him right if he got kicked in the head or something.

Nash's expression softened for a moment, but he quickly masked it with a curt nod. "Anyway, there might be something to investigate with these new bulls coming in. If that's the case, the closer I am to them, the better."

"Blevins has to be behind it. He's all about any press is good press. And these Mexican bulls are killers. Having them at the rodeo is going to bring up a lot of bad memories of last season when we lost Ronnie." Dolly still missed the sweet cowboy who would have been one of the sport's greatest riders had he lived after being thrown from an enraged steroid-injected bull.

"Looks like I've got two new situations to investigate. Let's hope that between the petting zoo and the fighting bulls, there's a connection…and something illegal I can pin on Blevins."

Before Dolly could respond, she caught sight of a familiar figure approaching their table. It was Mick Mickelson, a former cowboy whose career had ended after he took a bad fall from a bull. He had made it his life's mission to cause trouble for the UPRC, and her in particular, ever since. Was it too much to hope for that he'd get sidetracked by a beer or get hit in the head by a chair? She glanced over at the empty chair next to her, half considering it.

Mick sneered as he stood over them, arms crossed. "Look who we have here," he drawled, his gaze locked on Dolly. "The rodeo's very own spin doctor. I suppose you've got an answer for everything that's been going on?"

"What's been going on, Mick?" Nash asked, tensing. He met Mick's hostile gaze head-on.

"Plenty," Mick shot back, baring his teeth. "Like how

this rodeo's going to hell, and you two ain't doing nothing but making it worse. You with your shitty riding and her spray-painting glitter all over the horseshit show that counts as entertainment these days."

"Last I checked, you're not part of the UPRC anymore or welcome at any of the events," Dolly retorted, her patience wearing thin. She empathized that Mick's life wasn't going the way he had pictured it when he was a hotshot bull rider. But as he had also broken her baby sister LeAnn's heart, her empathy only went so far. "And while I realize that you need to feel relevant, stop trying to cause trouble for the rodeo or I'll put a restraining order on you so fast your head will spin."

"A restraining order is just a piece of paper," Mick said with an evil little smile she wanted to slap right off him.

"All right, that's enough," Nash growled, pushing back from the table and rising to his feet. His tall frame towered over Mick, but the former cowboy didn't flinch. They faced each other, locked in a tense standoff. "You want to leave right now before I break your other leg."

"I'd like to see you try."

Dolly saw several camera phones come out. Some of them were from Mick's friends who wouldn't know their way around social media with a flashlight and a map.

"Stand down, Nash. This is a setup."

"What?" he said, jerking his attention to her.

"Mick's trying to start something and get it on video so he can build up a following or go viral. He's looking for eight seconds of fame again. And he's not going to get it here."

Nash didn't like it, but he deliberately sat back down again.

"Coward," Mick spat.

Nash's jaw clenched and he glared at him but did nothing else.

That was enough of that. Dolly raised her own phone and pressed record. "Hi y'all," she said in a bright, happy voice. "I'm here at the Pig and Puddin' Palace in Killeen with up-and-coming bull rider Nash Weaver." She stood up and panned the camera over him. "Nash's mouth is full of delicious barbecue so he can't talk right now." Deliberately, she kept the camera off Mick and turned her back on him. "And look who else I see? It's Sammy Volero." She walked to one of Mick's cronies, who dropped his phone on the table when she centered him in her shot. "Sammy, I hear there are some Mexican fighting bulls coming into the lineup for next week's rodeo in Laredo. What do you think of that?"

As Sammy preened and stuttered, Dolly saw Mick seething behind her. After she moved on to his other friends, who were more than willing to talk on her live feed, he stormed away. Too bad. She had hoped to goad him into doing something stupid on camera.

When she finished up the post, she came back to the table. The live post had gotten some hearts and thumbs-up. Maybe she needed to do more lives before and after the rodeos. They seemed to be popular.

"Were you always so good at putting a spin on things?" Nash asked, scowling at her for some reason.

"It's a skill that's gotten me out of tight situations," she said.

"In my experience, people who bend the truth tend to bend the rules too."

Dolly gave a half-shrug. "Rules are made to be broken, don't you think?"

Nash winced. "No."

"Right." Dolly shook her head and whispered again, "Once a Fed always a Fed." Then a little louder she said, "I play by the rules when others play by them. But if you want a fair fight, sometimes you have to get down to their level."

Rolling his eyes, Nash got up and threw some cash on the table, more than enough to cover their meal. "Give me a call when Reba can get us in to see those bulls and you can do a photo shoot or something." Without another word, he stormed out of the restaurant.

As she watched him go, her emotions swirled with a mixture of worry and frustration. Dolly wished they could have a conversation that ended more pleasantly. Had he been mad that she hadn't let him duke it out with Mick? Or was he just done with the whole social media thing? Either way, she would have liked to have finished their meal with a shared peach pie or something. Maybe walk hand in hand into the sunset? A good-night peck on the cheek?

Well, to hell with him. She'd order dessert without him. While she waited for it to come out—with a scoop of ice cream—and while the thoughts of Mexican fighting bulls were still fresh in her mind, Dolly called LeAnn.

"Hey, what's up?" LeAnn said.

"I just overheard some rodeo hands talking about a shipment of Mexican fighting bulls coming in. I thought you should know since you're riding this season."

"Really?" LeAnn's enthusiasm didn't waver. If anything, it seemed to grow. "That's amazing. I've always wanted to try my hand at riding those beasts."

Dolly clenched her jaw, irritated by her sister's reckless attitude. "Those bulls are killers. This isn't something to celebrate."

"This is what bull riding is all about—facing danger head-on and coming out stronger for it."

"Right, because getting gored by a bull is really going to make you stronger," Dolly muttered under her breath, but she knew there was no use arguing with LeAnn when her adrenaline was up. "Just…be careful, all right?"

"Where's the fun in that?" LeAnn replied cheerily before hanging up.

Dolly sighed, slipping her phone back into her pocket. As she turned to leave the barbecue restaurant, she spotted another of her sisters, Loretta, sitting at a nearby table with Taylor. They were laughing together over plates piled high with brisket and coleslaw, seemingly oblivious to the world around them.

For a moment, Dolly felt a pang of longing. She wished she could have someone like that in her life. There just didn't seem to be anyone who fit into her world. Her thoughts flickered to Nash again. Anyone who was interested in her, anyway.

Still, she was glad for Loretta. Her sister had been through hell and back after discovering her rock star husband's infidelity and then after the divorce, falling for an art professor who turned out to be married with kids. If anyone deserved a fresh start, it was Loretta.

Dolly watched them for a moment longer, taking in the easy smiles and the warmth of their connection. Then she squared her shoulders, reminding herself that she had bigger fish to fry—like figuring out Jackson Blevins's true intentions and keeping her sisters safe from the fallout.

Chapter Six

Nash

IT WASN'T HARD to catch up to Mick in the parking lot. The man couldn't walk very fast with his shattered leg. As Nash closed the distance, Mick whirled, flicking open a switchblade.

"You're going to jump me when my back was turned?" he snarled.

"No," Nash said, holding out his hands placatingly. He knew he could disarm Mick and put him on his ass, but that wouldn't get them anywhere.

Now that Mick had lost his audience, he wasn't looking to perform anymore. Mick appeared to be exactly what he was: a down-on-his-luck former rodeo star with an axe to grind. An axe that might lead to chopping off Blevins's head for Shelby's proverbial platter.

"I wanted to talk to you about Kingmaker," Nash said.

"Go fuck yourself." And yet, Mick didn't move away. He also didn't put away the switchblade.

Kingmaker was the bull that Blevins had arranged to be provided to the women's rodeo when they were still a separate entity from the men's rodeo. LeAnn Keller should have been on it. For some dumb-ass reason, Mick had arranged to switch the bull he had chosen to ride that day for her bull, Templar. If he hadn't, LeAnn's career would have been over, and Mick would still be on the roster.

"Who switched Kingmaker and Templar?" Nash asked.

"Why does it matter now?" Mick shook his head. "I paid two hundred dollars to wreck and ruin my life."

"Who did you pay the money to?"

"Why—are you looking to switch bulls with someone?" Mick got a crafty look in his eye.

Sure. Let's go with that. "Yeah."

Mick nodded and pulled out a cigarette. He lit it up. "I figured you're looking for an easy ride. But they got the doc that was sticking the bulls with 'roids. If you think Reba's going to stick yours with a sedative, you're crazy."

Nash decided to play a hunch. "Reba doesn't have to know."

Taking a long drag from the cigarette, Mick contemplated the burning tip before slowly blowing it out. "I might be able to hook you up with someone who can switch a bull at the last minute. But I don't know or want to know anything about drugging the bulls."

Nash believed him. Which was a shame, since he had a feeling he'd sing like a canary if Nash applied some pressure. He peeled off two one-hundred-dollar bills, and he offered them to Mick.

"A little more than that," Mick said with a nasty grin.

Nash added one more hundred to the pile. "Take it or leave it."

Mick took it. "You want to talk to Ryan Chester. Don't

tell him I sent you."

Turning away from Mick, Nash headed over to his truck. He was racking his brain for any information on Ryan Chester. The name sounded familiar. He needed to go back to his motel room and take a look at his board. He probably should keep it all electronic, but it helped to stare at it at night and move things around on it.

The motel was as far away from the rodeo as he could get without being inconvenienced too much. He didn't want to encourage any visitors, not that anyone had really gone out of their way to invite him out for a drink or a party.

When he let himself in, the silence of his room was only broken by the soft hum of the air-conditioning unit. The small desk before him was cluttered with papers and a laptop. A single window looked out onto the empty parking lot, offering no comfort or distraction from the task at hand. This cramped space served as a makeshift headquarters for his investigation. The room felt suffocating, the air thick with isolation and the weight of responsibility bearing down. The motel walls seemed to close in as he sifted through bank statements and emails, searching for any clue that might bring him closer to exposing the truth.

He almost missed the crowds and the hustle and bustle of the day's rodeo. He definitely missed the days when he could rely on the FBI's resources to aid him in his investigations. But those days were gone, and so were the connections he'd once taken for granted. His retirement had severed those ties, leaving him to navigate this new world as a private investigator with little more than his wits and determination. He stared at a spreadsheet detailing bank transactions, his mind's eye flicking back to his time with the bureau. Miles Garrett, his former partner, would have taken shortcuts, bending rules to get the information he needed.

And he'd probably have gotten away with it. Nash scowled. Well, not him. Nash would do it the old-fashioned way, pure research and hard work. Turning his attention to Ryan Chester, Nash opened up the files on all the employees of the UPRC rodeo. As he scrolled through their portfolios, he paused when Dolly's face appeared on the screen. Her blue eyes seemed to sparkle even in the static image, drawing him in despite himself.

Nash couldn't help but linger on her past at Leisure Industries, the escort service she'd worked for briefly before finding stability in her current role. A wave of jealousy surged through him as he thought of the men who had been her clients, though he quickly pushed the feeling away, reminding himself that it was long before they'd met.

He frowned, trying to understand why Dolly's family hadn't stepped in to help her during those dark days. He hoped that once they got to know each other better, she'd trust him with that story.

It wasn't productive to get so distracted, but Dolly had a way of creeping into his thoughts when he least expected it. Her smile, the sound of her laughter, the sweet perfume she wore that made his mind immediately think about sex. Being with her made him want things he'd never dared to dream of before. A life beyond the job, beyond the shadows that had always dogged his steps. But was the attraction he sensed from her real? If she had been an escort, she must have been very good at making men believe she really liked them.

Maybe there would be time for Dolly later, once Blevins was behind bars and Shelby was safe. Right now, he had to stay sharp, follow each clue to its end. No matter where it led him. Could it lead him to Dolly and her brother-in-law? Was she just interested in this investigation and him because she wanted to stay one step ahead? His gut said no. But he didn't quite trust his gut fully on this. His gut had also told him to report Miles Garrett's harmless but still illegal investigations. In the end, the only one who had been really punished for that had been Nash.

Forcing himself to move on, Nash delved deeper into Ryan Chester: twenty-nine, single, born in Austin. Hired two years ago to oversee livestock.

Nash peered closer at the copy of Ryan's employee ID. The photo was blurry, but unless he missed his guess, that tattoo on Ryan's neck wasn't just any tribal design. Where had he seen it before?

He shuffled through his notes and the pictures on his phone. There. On the shipping label were three interlocked Rs inside a diamond. The Rocky Ridge Ranch brand. That was the Canadian stock supplier where Donnan was from. Chester had their brand on his neck. If that wasn't shades of the television show *Yellowstone*, Nash didn't know what was. It could also be a connection. If Ryan was willing to do questionable things for extra cash, maybe Blevins knew that and was exploiting it somehow.

With renewed focus, Nash examined Ryan Chester's work schedule and personal information. He wondered if he could sneak around and check out Ryan's truck during the rodeo next weekend. He snapped a picture of Ryan's employee ID so he could refer to it later. Then he also searched for people hired around the same time as Ryan to add them to his list of people to watch out for.

He jotted down a note to also talk to Taylor Keating about what he had been buying today. Could be nothing. Could be another clue to follow.

The next stock supplier on his list of suspects was the Jaripeo Ranch. No surprise that they were supplying the new shipment of fighting bulls. He scrolled through the contracts and their employees. He found a connection. Hector Ortiz, who was a current UPRC employee, had been hired around the same time as Ryan Chester. Hector had formerly been employed at Jaripeo Ranch in Guanajuato. No neck tattoo or brand that he could see, though. So probably no connections between those two. But they both moved up a bit on his suspect list.

Then he reluctantly brought up Shane Calland and the Viking Ranch. He didn't like looking at Dolly's brother-in-law for this, but he had to be thorough. Shane was a hothead and shared the Keller family's dislike of Blevins, but Nash wanted to make sure he wasn't discounting him because of Nash's feelings for Dolly.

Nash's eyes were burning and he couldn't look at his computer or his board any longer. He needed to actually do something. If he was going to get fired tomorrow, he should make the most of his credentials now while he was still a part of the UPRC. It wasn't too late to go back to the rodeo and look around and see if there was anything in the Rocky Ridge or Jaripeo areas that could be a clue. This time of night, the cowboys would be getting their drink on and not paying too much attention to the barns. Prime time to sneak around and maybe he'd get lucky and find something to pin on Ryan Chester or Hector Ortiz.

Chapter Seven

Dolly

IT HAD BEEN a long first day to the start of the rodeo season. Dolly wished she were back in her apartment in Dallas instead of spending the night in the Winnebago, but she was right to have planned for not wanting to drive the two hours home. She could barely afford the apartment, but she needed to be close to headquarters when the rodeos weren't in session. Jefferson Laker's hundred grand hadn't lasted as long as Dolly had imagined it would. Five years later, it was all gone and she was trying not to live paycheck to paycheck. She got some residual payments from her old YouTube videos and, every now and then, she'd pull in a paid sponsor for her personal Instagram account. Mostly, though, they just sent boxes of crap that they hoped she would promote for free on her channel.

The scent of Loretta's oil paints mingling with the ever-present aroma of the rodeo grounds and old coffee was comforting in its own way. The RV was her family's second home, and she knew she should relish the quiet of being alone. With a family as big as hers, it didn't happen often.

Still, she was feeling restless and she wasn't ready for

bed just yet. Loretta still hadn't come home from her first date with Taylor, and Dolly didn't want to do any more social media work while she waited up. She was starting to doom scroll and she knew from past experience that was a path she didn't want to go down.

She could call her other sisters and see what they were up to. But Reba was probably tired from her shift at the rodeo and was likely snuggled up with Shane at the moment. LeAnn and Dylan were probably out partying. Dolly considered getting all dolled up and hitting the clubs with them, but she didn't want to be a third wheel. Besides, it was just too exhausting to be "on" right now. Her face hurt from smiling and she didn't feel like putting on the act that everything in her life was Instagram-perfect.

Blevins was blowing up her phone again. He wanted her to meet him in his office next week so they could discuss more marketing ideas. Luckily, Shelby was running interference for her by telling him that she needed Dolly at the rodeos. Still, Dolly's luck was going to run out when she was back in the office on Monday. Maybe, she could do a little investigating of her own by pretending to be interested in his nonsense. Who knew what he might slip up and say? She grimaced at the thought of being alone with him. Maybe she could keep the door open or invite Shelby to join them. When she'd told Shelby about Blevins being creepy, Shelby had told her to keep a log and screenshots for evidence. So far, he hadn't crossed any lines.

A loud fast knock on the Winnebago's door startled her. She glanced at the clock. It was almost eleven. Who the heck could that be? Her sisters would have just barged right on in. They all had keys. Dolly peeked through the curtain and saw a figure hurrying away. Opening the door, she was going to call out to them but then noticed there was a gift-wrapped package on the RV's step.

Bending down, she picked it up and brought it inside. It was addressed to her. She wondered if it was a swag bag from someone who wanted her to promote their goods on social media. Dolly hoped it was food, preferably something with peanut butter and chocolate.

She admired the wrapping, running her fingers over the thick, glossy black paper. This was the good stuff. Maybe she should do an unboxing video? Nah, she could always wrap it back up if it was out of the ordinary. If it was stickers, bandanas, or T-shirts, she didn't want to waste the effort.

Maybe it was a gift from an admirer? She shook the package and peered at it from all angles. Would Nash have given her a present to apologize for leaving so abruptly? Dolly snorted. Yeah, that would be the day.

She carefully unwrapped the gift, making sure not to tear the wrapping. After sliding the box out of the paper, Dolly opened it up. She had to sit down before she fell down. Inside was a Dallas Cowboy Cheerleader uniform, but that wasn't what filled her with dread. A business card from Leisure Industries was pinned to the skimpy blue top. With shaking fingers, she picked it up. Turning it over she saw that it said, "How much?" in block letters.

Son of a bitch.

She crumpled the business card up in her fist. Who the hell could have done this? Finn? She grabbed the uniform and checked the tags and the seams. It was authentic. Something a billionaire could easily afford and obtain—or a billionaire's son.

Dolly ran out of the Winnebago, grabbing the baseball bat that she kept by the door. She sprinted in the direction she saw the figure go, but it was dark out and she was in the rodeo parking lot. Gripping the bat, she glared all around her, but she didn't see anyone skulking around or hiding.

A truck door slammed nearby, and she nearly jumped out of her skin.

"You all right?"

Dolly recognized Nash's voice and just barely stopped herself from swinging.

"Whoa, slugger. What's going on?"

She would not cry. She would not cry.

"Dolly?" Nash's voice was concerned. "Talk to me."

She dropped the bat and launched herself into his arms.

"Okay. Okay," he soothed as she clung to him.

Dolly held on tightly as he rubbed her back.

"You're shaking. Come on, let's get you inside." He moved toward the Winnebago.

No. She couldn't let him see the uniform and have him start asking questions about why someone thought it was okay to send it to her and expect her to wear it for him. Tomorrow, she could spin the story into something that would hide her escort past. But right now, Dolly was too raw to think up anything on the fly.

"I'm fine. I just got a scare," she said. She refused to let him go. It felt nice to be held in his strong, protective arms.

"Do I have to beat the shit out of someone?"

She hiccupped a laugh that horrifyingly sounded close to a sob. "Get in line."

"Seriously, I'm in the mood to kick someone's ass."

Rubbing her cheek against the soft flannel of his shirt, Dolly sighed. She had to tell him something. He was an investigator after all. He was going to keep probing and questioning until she gave him something. "It's all right. I probably overreacted. Someone left a gift on my doorstep and I got offended." That wasn't even remotely close to the truth, but it should buy her some time.

He tensed up. "What kind of gift?"

Dolly should have known he wouldn't let it drop. Taking in a shaky breath, she forced herself to leave the safety of his arms. It was tough. But she needed to put on her big-girl panties and woman up. She was all right. It was probably just a shitty practical joke. Although, when her brain tried to convince herself of that, she immediately saw the holes in that logic. "I don't want to go into it right now."

"Do you want me to take a look at it?"

"No." Dolly shook her head and bent down to pick up her bat. "It's nothing."

"It's not nothing, if it upset you."

She was having a hard time not spilling her guts to him. It was especially rough when he looked so concerned and handsome at the same time.

"I'm fine." Dolly decided she needed a little misdirection to take his mind off her problems. "What are you doing back here at this hour?"

"I wanted to take a second look around the rodeo after dark."

"Why?" she asked suspiciously. Could Nash have dropped off the "gift"? Nah, she was just being paranoid.

"I figured now would be a good chance to look around without prying eyes."

"Good point," she said. "We might find something Blevins or his cronies left behind when he wasn't expecting company."

"Me. Not we."

"I should come along. I could be a good lookout or hold the flashlight or something."

"Absolutely not," he shot back, his jaw clenched. "It's too risky. If we get caught, you could get in trouble, and I can't let that happen."

"Excuse me?" Dolly bristled, indignant at the implication that she couldn't handle herself. "If we get caught, I'm pretty sure I can talk us out of it."

"Can you really?" Nash challenged.

"Have you met me?" Dolly folded her arms across her chest. "I could charm the spots off a leopard."

He grunted in agreement. "It's not exactly legal, poking around like we're going to do."

"Neither is whatever Blevins's doing," Dolly countered.

"I've got Shelby's permission to do what it takes. That permission doesn't apply to you."

"So what?"

Dolly watched as Nash's jaw worked.

"You might need the backup," she cajoled.

"Fine," he finally conceded. "But we're doing this my

way. Being careful."

"I always am," Dolly assured him, though her history suggested otherwise.

Nash regarded her for a long moment. Finally, he sighed, nodding in reluctant agreement. "Stay close to me, understand? I don't want anything happening to you."

"Deal," she agreed. "We should check on all the animals. Make sure there isn't anything funny going on with them," she said.

"Isn't that Reba's job?"

"Yeah, but she's not there at night."

"Okay. I guess that's a good of a place to start as any."

Dolly wasn't sure she'd be able to spot a drugged animal, unless they were acting weird. But going out with Nash right now would be a nice distraction for her too. She didn't really want to be alone right now. Doing something productive might make her feel a little better. Not to mention, she might get a chance to hug Nash again.

"Give me a few minutes and I'll join you."

"I don't..." He started to say more, but she was already rushing back to the Winnebago.

Dolly pushed open the door to her Winnebago, bracing herself for the fear and anger she'd feel when she looked at the uniform. She stepped inside and stopped short at the sight of Loretta and Taylor hastily jumping apart—their flushed cheeks and tousled hair evidence of what they had been up to. They must have come back while she was out.

Dolly's gaze slid to the gift that she had left on the table. They hadn't seemed to notice it. Likely, they'd been too distracted.

"I didn't mean to interrupt," Dolly drawled.

She didn't bother hiding her amusement, but she knew better than to push too hard. Loretta deserved her happiness, even if it came wrapped in secrecy and stolen moments. Dolly sidled over to the table, hoping to keep their attention off the contents of the package.

"Um, yeah," Loretta stammered, her cheeks flushed. "We were just...talking."

"Sure," Dolly replied, smirking as she located her sneakers beneath the small kitchen table. She picked them up and nonchalantly scooped up the package from the table. "I'm actually on my way back out. I just came back to change my shoes."

After stuffing the package under her bed, Dolly kicked off her sandals and put on her sneakers. Swiping a hand over her face, she was proud there weren't any tears. She'd figure out who send that awful gift tomorrow. Right now, she was going to get her Nancy Drew on. After grabbing a light jacket, she slid her bedroom door closed and headed for the door.

"Is everything okay?" Taylor asked, concern etching lines across his face, his eyes darting between the sisters.

"Yeah, great." Dolly shot Loretta a knowing look. "Just don't do anything I wouldn't do, all right?"

Her sister nodded, her expression a mix of gratitude and embarrassment. With a final smirk, Dolly left them alone to finish what they had started. She hoped that Taylor wouldn't break her sister's heart. She'd hate to have to break his face.

Dolly was glad that Nash was still where she had left

him. "I figured you'd be long gone by now."

"You would just follow me," he said. "And it's hard to sneak around when someone is actively looking for you."

"Smart man," Dolly said.

"What's going on?" Nash looked at her curiously.

"Why?" she asked.

"You're all flushed and you've got a scowl on your face. Something to do with this gift you received?"

She really wished he would forget about that. "No. It seems while I was out here, my sister just came back from her dinner date. I walked in on them making out. I guess I need to stay out a few more hours to give them the time they need to finish what they started." She shook her head, bemused. "She could have given me a heads-up or something. A text. A scarf on the doorknob. A little warning?"

"Maybe she got carried away," he said.

"I worry about her."

"I get it. I worry about my sister, too."

Dolly nodded. "Yeah, you're a good brother."

"Not really," he said. "But I'm trying to be. Let's get going. We stick together, and if anything feels off, we get out of there. I'm not expecting anything dramatic to happen, but you never know."

"Agreed," she said. "I have no plans to be a hero."

Was it her imagination or did he step closer to her? His aftershave teased her nostrils and she wanted to say to heck with sneaking around in the dark. They should go have a beer or two and see where the night led after that.

No. She took a step back. No. That was not why they were here. No matter how tempting it was. He was one phone call away from having his friends in the FBI doing a background check on her that could end everything. Since her sisters LeAnn and Reba had vouched for her, Shelby had only done a cursory reference check. Nepotism FTW!

As long as Dolly kept being helpful and keeping on everyone's good side, she should be able to get out of this situation with Blevins being kicked out and her past as an escort remaining hidden.

Still, was it too much to ask for a little more TLC? Dolly was still feeling a little raw about the uniform.

Chapter Eight

Dolly

THE KILLEEN RODEO Grounds were a different world after hours. The raucous energy of the day gave way to shadow and hush as they got farther away from the parking lot. Storage areas stood like silent sentinels beneath a moon that draped everything in silver-blue light. She and Nash crept toward them, shining the lights from their cell phones to guide their way.

"Each of the stock contractors has their own shed in each of the rodeos. I've made it a point to look through each of them at every event. I haven't found anything yet, but all it takes is one time for someone to mess up."

"Feels like we're the bad guys," Dolly whispered, her voice barely carrying over the muted sounds of livestock shuffling in their pens, the occasional snort or hoof-stomp punctuating the stillness.

Nash nodded, his gaze never ceasing its vigilant sweep of the area.

"Are you looking for anything specific?" she asked.

He hesitated, and she felt a flicker of annoyance that he was debating on what to tell her. "I know who switched

Mick's bull with LeAnn's last year. It was a guy named Ryan Chester. He's with the Rocky Ridge Ranch."

"That's Donnan's ranch. The Canadian one."

"Yeah. I was searching his truck when I saw you come flying out of your RV."

"Did you find anything to link him to Blevins?"

"Nope. All I found was he likes to chew, and he has a collection of *Penthouse*s under his truck seat."

Dolly wondered if this Ryan dude was the one who planted the uniform on her step. But liking stroke magazines didn't necessarily link him to Leisure Industries. The person who left her the gift was probably long gone, but the hairs on the back of her neck tingled, as if someone was watching them.

Flicking off her light, she eased against one of the sheds.

"Everything all right?"

"I'm not sure. Turn off your light and come here. I think someone is following us."

He pocketed his phone, and stood in front of her in the shadow of the building.

"You make a better door than a window," she whispered and stepped to the side so she could see around his bulk. As they stood there in the stillness of the warm night, Dolly resisted the urge to sway into him and lean on him again for support.

After a few minutes, Nash said, "There's no one there."

"Yeah, I must be imagining things."

"You can't be too careful."

She nodded and they continued to the Rocky Ridge's

shed. Still, she couldn't shake the feeling that something was off.

"Do you know anything about Ryan Chester?" Nash asked as he fiddled with the lock on the door.

"No."

"I thought you knew everyone," he said with a grin.

"I could try and get to know him," she said. "I could say I'm doing a reel on Donnan's home ranch."

"Maybe," Nash said. "I want to be with you, though, when you approach him."

Dolly wanted to be annoyed, because she could handle herself, but she understood that he needed to do his job too. She watched as he manipulated the lock using two long metal picks. "They teach you that in the FBI?"

Nash gave her a grim smile. "Dad taught Shelby and me that when we were kids."

Closing her eyes, Dolly wished that the earth would open up and swallow her. "Sorry."

He popped the lock open. "It has its uses. The bureau taught me how to bypass the electronic locks."

The storage door opened with a loud creak that had them wincing and looking around. It was early enough that anyone who would be sleeping on site to watch over the animals would still be out and about. But luckily, it was late enough that the only people around were her and Nash.

"What are we looking for?" Dolly said as she walked in.

Nash closed the door behind them.

For a moment, they were in pitch-blackness with only their cell phone lights to see. But then he pulled on a dangling string and a bare bulb dimly lit up the area.

"Anything out of the ordinary," he said, going over to the shelving units.

"How about this?" She gestured toward a stack of hay bales that weren't in a tidy stack like the rest of them.

"Could be something. Could be nothing," he said.

But as they approached, she noticed that the floor around the askew bales was cleaner than the rest of the area.

"Looks like someone swept up a mess." Nash hauled the heavy bales aside with a grunt while she held the light steady on the floor to get a better look.

"There's something there." She crouched down and wiped her hand across the floor until a latch was revealed. "This looks like a secret compartment."

"It's definitely a compartment," he said. "But I'm not getting my hopes up that it's secret. It could just be storage."

"Or Rocky Ridge is smuggling things in from Canada and leaving them here for Blevins to pick up," she said, feeling a prick of eagerness shake through her.

"Don't jump to conclusions," he said.

"Have you seen anything like this in the other sheds at the other rodeos?" she challenged.

"No, but I haven't been moving hale bales around either. It's your find. You can open the compartment."

This time, he held the light while Dolly pulled up on the latch. They both peered into the space. There was enough room there to store a few shoe boxes of stuff, but at the moment, it was empty.

"Well, shit," she said.

"Looks like whatever was here is gone now," Nash said. "But it's been recently used, based on how clean it is. That's what we would call a clue in the FBI."

"Hidden compartments are probable cause, right?"

"Not exactly," he said, obviously amused by her television cop lingo.

"I wonder if they have a hidey-hole in all the rodeo sheds." Dolly stood, brushing her hands against her jeans, a determined glint in her eye. "Are we going to stake them out?"

"There is no *we* in this," he said. "I'll see about setting up some discreet surveillance cameras in here and in Laredo's storage areas for next week's rodeo. I'll wire this one up for any action tomorrow, just in case. But I think we missed our opportunity to find out what this is being used for."

Dolly snapped a few photographs. "For evidence."

"Keep it off social media and don't tell anyone about this."

"I'm not an idiot," she said icily.

"I know that," he said.

He closed the compartment and moved the hay bales back to approximately where they were. Nash reached out to remove a piece of straw from her hair. "I just want you to be careful. Blevins is dangerous and so are the people he's dealing with. I might not know exactly what they're up to, but I'm sure they'll go to extremes to protect their interests."

"Why do I feel like this is all coming to a head?" she asked. Shivers made goose bumps up and down her arms.

"Because you've got good instincts."

She swallowed hard as they drifted closer. The feeling to dive back into his arms was a powerful one. The quiet of the night was peaceful and she wanted him more than she had any right to.

"Can I trust you, Nash?"

"Depends."

That wasn't the answer she was looking for, but she admired his honesty. She couldn't trust him with her secrets. Not yet anyway.

"N-next unit," she stuttered and shuffled by him out the door before he could read the desire in her eyes.

Together they slipped back into the shadows, moving on toward the next building. A lot could fit in that compartment, if the Rocky Ridge Ranch was smuggling stuff across the border. Pills, powder, drugs of all sorts. But it could also just be extra storage.

"I'll text Shane and ask him if he's got that same compartment in his barn," she said.

"No, don't," Nash said.

"He'd know if that was a standard space to have in the floor." She started to text.

"I said, no." Nash put his hand over her phone.

"What?" She stared up at him and then realized he still thought the Viking Ranch might be a part of this. Dolly scowled at him. "Shane can help us. We can trust him. He's family."

"Not yet he's not."

"Reba trusts him and Shelby trusts Reba. You're wasting your time suspecting him."

"The Viking Ranch unit is right there." Nash pointed. "No sense bothering him. We can look ourselves. No sense tipping him off either."

"Shane isn't involved with Blevins," she said through her teeth.

"Then he won't mind if we have a little look around."

This was why she couldn't get involved with Nash. He was a suspicious bastard, and he was too stubborn to realize that he was wrong about Shane. She angrily helped him toss hay bales around, but there wasn't a floor compartment in either the Viking Ranch's or the Rocky Ridge Ranch's storage area. She wasn't annoyed anymore, but her back ached something fierce.

Once they were done with the sheds, they had to pass by the pens where the bulls were bedded down for the night. They were restless silhouettes against the weathered wood of their enclosures, their breaths sending up plumes of mist that caught the moonlight. One bull, larger than the others, paced back and forth, its massive head swinging as if to challenge the darkness itself.

"Those beasts are nothing but muscle and mean," Nash observed, peering through the slats at the agitated creatures. Their eyes glinted, reflecting a primal anger that no night could soothe.

"Yeah, and you want to ride one," Dolly murmured, her gaze following the movement of the bull.

"Want is a strong word."

"LeAnn can't wait to try her luck on one of the Mexican fighting bulls. The meaner the better."

"She got a death wish?"

"I don't know what she's got. Ambition with a healthy dose of insanity. Do you see the appeal of it?" Dolly looked up at him.

He thought about it for a moment. "Do you like roller coasters?"

"Sure, but I wouldn't if there was a chance I'd get flung off them."

"It adds to the excitement. Don't get me wrong—the landing on the hard ground tempers the excitement a bit. But it can be fun."

"Fun," Dolly said flatly.

"Well, what do you do for fun?"

"Nothing that's going to get me killed," she retorted.

"But you do like the adrenaline rush of doing something like this."

"What girl wouldn't?" she said, nudging him with her elbow. "It adds a little spice to my dull life."

"Your life isn't dull."

"The life I let you see isn't dull," she said and then could have clamped her hand over her mouth. What was it about him that made all her guarded walls crumble?

"You don't have to hide who you really are."

She gave an unladylike snort. "I do if I want ad revenue and views."

"There's more to life than that."

"Well of course there is, Captain Obvious, but clicks pay my bills. And it can all go away so fast." She stared out into the darkness and tried not to feel the panic creeping up on her from the shadows. "After I left cheerleading…after my contract wasn't renewed, I tried to make a living online doing makeup tutorials. I spent way too much money on high-end cosmetics with pretty bottles and decorative sets. I was doing great and then one day, I left a used tissue on the counter and it was in my shot. That was all anyone commented on in the video." She shook her head. "It took a month to regain the likes and followers. So I learned to show the world perfect."

"You're not on camera now," he said. "And I think you're perfect just the way you are."

Dolly gaped up at him. He wouldn't if he knew the truth about her past. "Then why am I listed as Pain in The Ass on your phone?"

His lips twisted. "I didn't know you saw that."

"Again. I'm not an idiot, Nash."

"You can be a PITA and be perfect at the same time."

"I think you have a weird definition of perfect."

"Well, then I guess I'm not perfect either."

"Is that why you retired early from the FBI?"

It was his turn to stare out into the darkness. "No."

"Have you ever thought about what you'd be doing, if you hadn't left?"

"Every day since I left."

"Then why did you?"

"Long story," he said, turning away from her.

"Sad one, by the looks of it."

"I'm more angry than sad. I was forced out. Basically, I followed the rules and it came back to bite me in the ass."

She glanced down and back. "It's a nice ass." *No. Dolly. No.* She had to stop flirting with him. It wouldn't end well.

"Thanks," he said, with a small smile. "But there's no

sense dwelling on it. If I was out on assignment with the bureau, then I couldn't be here, helping Shelby."

"Guess not," she said. "And I wouldn't have met such a charming cowboy."

"Charming is a stretch," he replied dryly. "So is cowboy."

"Private investigator, then."

"Better."

"You and Shelby must be close."

"We've had to be with our parents being the people they are."

"My sisters and I are close too."

"How many do you have anyway?" he asked.

"There's four of us. Loretta is the only one not really involved in the rodeo. This is the first season she's been with the UPRC. You might have seen her selling her paintings along vendor row. She's really good. She's going to be living with me in the Winnebago this season when we're on the road."

"That must cramp your style."

"I think I'm cramping her style," Dolly muttered.

"What?"

"She's seeing Taylor Keating. That's who she was kissing tonight."

"Taylor, huh?" Nash looked thoughtful.

"He's the bullfighter who sometimes rides if the purse is big enough and he can wheedle his way onto the docket for the day."

"How well do you know Taylor?"

Uh-oh. "Why? You don't think he's involved in whatever Blevins has his hands in, do you?"

That was all Loretta needed.

"I told you. I suspect everyone."

"Well, if he is dirty, I'd appreciate a heads-up. I hope he's not, though. Loretta could use a break. She hasn't had a whole lot of luck with men."

"How about you?"

She gave him a double take. "I'm not an asshole magnet like Loretta is. But I've been concentrating on this job and building my own brand. There hasn't been a lot of time for romance." After the escort service, Dolly had had a hard time casual dating. She always wondered if the men she went out with were doing a mental tally in their head of how much they had to spend on her before she would sleep with them. Dinner $100. Drinks $50. It was cynical and she hated thinking like that, but she also couldn't stop herself.

"For me either."

"That so?"

Nash had never made her feel like a commodity. Pissed her off? Sure. Was he the leading man in her lonely week-night fantasies? Absolutely. That was why she was a little scared of getting involved with him. He could really hurt her feelings if he rejected her because of her past.

The tension between them was like an electric current that buzzed over her skin. This time, she definitely wasn't imagining that they were drifting closer together. Almost close enough to kiss…

"Hey, what are you two doing there?" A loud voice startled her out of the sensuous haze she was dropping into.

Dolly jumped back and placed a hand over her heart. Nash whirled to confront the man who was stalking toward them. Luckily, she recognized Shane's assistant Pat gripping a tire iron in his hand.

"Pat, it's me—Dolly. I'm looking for Reba," she blurted out.

Pat nearly tripped, he stopped in his tracks so fast. "Oh shit, Dolly. I didn't recognize you. Shane and Reba are in the hotel tonight. It's my night to babysit the bulls."

Ever since Shane's bulls were tampered with, he'd made it a point to have one of his employees with them at all times. She hadn't thought he'd be this close.

"Oh, that's okay. I don't want to bother them. I'll catch up with Reba tomorrow. How are things going tonight?"

"Quiet," Pat said and stifled a yawn. "I thought things were about to get interesting when I saw the two of you."

They were about to get interesting, just not in the way that Pat meant it.

"Have you seen other people wandering around tonight?" Nash asked, and she could have kicked him.

Pat narrowed his eyes at him. "Aren't you one of the bull riders?"

Dolly grabbed Nash's hand. "He's with me."

Pat's eyes widened. "Oh. Oh. OH." He drawled out the last word. "I'm sorry for interrupting, then."

"No, it's okay," she said, feeling the blush hit her face hard. She was going to have to do a lot of explaining to Reba tomorrow. "We were just going."

"You have a good night, then."

Dolly dragged Nash by the hand away from the bulls

and from Pat who was grinning his fool head off.

"I wanted to know what he was going to say," Nash complained.

"I'll get the dirt for you tomorrow when I talk to Reba. She'll know if there's anyone who has been wandering around after hours."

She could tell by the way Nash twisted his lips that he wasn't happy about involving Shane and Reba in the investigation, but that was too damned bad. Reba knew who Nash was and Shelby trusted her. That should be enough to clear the Viking Ranch from suspicion. It torqued her off that it didn't.

Chapter Nine

Nash

THE INTIMATE MOMENT between them was lost. That was probably a good thing, considering where they were. And yet his lips still tingled from the phantom contact of the kiss that never happened. Nash had been so close to kissing her, and he was having a hard time getting his head back into the investigation. All he wanted to do was sling his arm around her and buy her a drink at an upscale bar. She deserved something like that, rather than poking around after dark hoping not to step in horseshit or something.

The tension between them lingered in the air as they made their way back toward the parking lot. Despite the interruption and the awkwardness that followed, Nash couldn't shake the feeling of longing that had surged through him during their almost kiss. His mind raced with conflicting thoughts—wanting to protect Dolly from any potential harm that may come their way as they delved deeper into the investigation while also battling the desire to keep her close, to feel that electric connection once more. Hopefully, this case wouldn't be going on for too much longer. Nash believed that they were getting closer to unraveling the mystery of what Blevins was up to. He knew, though, that once they did catch a break, Jackson Blevins might not go down easily. He wanted Dolly out of the picture long before that happened.

And as much as he hated prematurely crossing suspects off the list, he had a feeling that investigating Shane Calland and the Viking Ranch wouldn't lead to anything. Which left him with Taylor Keating, Hector Ortiz from the Jaripeo Ranch, and Ryan Chester from the Rocky Ridge Ranches as his main leads to follow. He'd make it a point to talk to them as soon as tomorrow after he got back from Dallas to see his sister.

"What made you decide to be a private investigator?" Dolly blurted out, as if she was trying too hard to break through the awkwardness.

"I like the challenge of figuring out puzzles. I didn't want to work for anyone else again. So doing this allows me to be my own boss."

"Make your own rules?"

"And make sure the rules get followed."

A pained look crossed Dolly's face. "Sometimes you have to break the rules or bend them a bit."

"Now you sound like my father."

"Ouch," she said. "He did a number on you, didn't he?"

"He did indeed."

"You were never tempted to find him? I mean with all the resources that the FBI has..."

"No." Nash didn't mean to cut her off, but he also

didn't want to hear it out loud. He heard it in his own brain often enough. And whenever he had to speak to his mother.

But when Dolly blinked at him in shock, he realized that it had come out harsher than she deserved to be on the receiving end of. She wasn't Miles, after all.

"It's illegal to do that unless he's a suspect in an investigation," he said in what he thought was a more reasonable tone.

"From what you said, he's probably a suspect in someone's investigation."

"But not mine. I'm not going to chase him all over the world." The last thing he had heard was his father was pretending to be a member of the royal family of some obscure country that sounded feasible enough to allow him free room and board all over Europe.

"Even if it meant you could find him and maybe stop him from hurting anyone else?"

"You sound a lot like my mother right now."

"That sounds like an insult," she said, a small note of hurt in her voice.

He was fucking this up. Badly. Dolly had no idea she was pushing all his buttons. "You'd understand if you ever met her."

"Do you see her often?"

Nash shook his head. "She's toxic."

"I'm sorry." She laid a hand on his arm. "If you ever want, you're welcome to join me and my sisters for some family time. It's chaotic, noisy, and loud as hell. But no one is toxic."

"Thanks," he said.

"I bet you were a good agent."

"I tried to be." Not good enough, though.

"It sounds like it was exciting. How does being a PI compare?"

"It has its moments, that's for sure. This is about as exciting as it gets. Most of this job is paperwork and computer time, not just skulking around in the dark with a beautiful woman."

Dolly smiled at that, so maybe he'd managed to salvage the situation.

"The trail leading to Blevins and what he's up to is finally narrowing down." He jerked his thumb behind them. "Victor Lance knows more than he's saying. But he's too afraid of Blevins to spill the beans. The Mexican fighting bulls or the petting zoo are new ventures that could be a front for smuggling or racketeering. While it would be nice to catch Blevins red-handed, the more likely way this is going down is through research and dumb luck."

"Sounds like my job too, sifting through tons of social media content to find that one viral post. Don't forget, I can do some digging online too if you need me to research something. Two heads are better than one."

"I don't want you to risk your job for this. I know how busy you are. You've got to make me look good after all."

"I'm not going to have to work all that hard." She gestured to where the petting zoo was locked up tight for the night. "Donnan over there is going to make you an internet sensation. While we're here, we should check on him."

"Might as well."

The petting zoo loomed like a child's playroom abandoned at dusk, scattered with the shapes of miniature animals sleeping or shifting restlessly in their enclosures. Miniature goats nestled together for warmth, a solitary donkey stood stoically by the fence, and fluffy rabbits burrowed into the hay.

"Looks peaceful," Dolly murmured, her flashlight beam dancing across the little signs that listed information about each animal.

"Doesn't seem like Blevins's style to put together a petting zoo for kids out of the blue," Nash said. "I wonder what he's really up to here."

"His style is more like mud wrestling pigs or something."

"Not that there's anything wrong with that." Nash grinned.

"As long as everyone consents," Dolly said, "I'm fine with it. I just don't want to promote it."

They inspected the floors, but it didn't look like there were any secret compartments hastily covered up by straw. Donnan was sleeping peacefully by a larger version of himself. The goats bleated softly as they passed by. They moved on by where the pygmy pigs were snuggled up for the night. "No hidden diamonds in their pen that I can see. No bags of drugs crammed in between the feed bags. I'm beginning to get discouraged," Dolly said.

"This is a dead end," he said. "We should go. It's getting late."

When they left the petting zoo, they had to pass by one of the horse barns to get back to where the Winnebago was parked. Nash trailed behind, his eyes never leaving her figure as she moved with a sexy sway.

"That's not supposed to be like that," she said, pointing toward one of the horse barns. The door was hanging open. "Let's go check it out." She tugged his hand and pulled him in the direction of the building.

"Careful," he murmured as Dolly's boot caught on a tractor rut just before the entrance. Her body lurched forward precariously.

He grabbed her to him, to steady her.

"Whoops," she breathed, her tone a mixture of relief and something richer, more potent. They were close, too close, and yet not nearly close enough. The warmth from her body seeped into his, a welcome heat in the coolness of the Texan night.

"Thanks," Dolly managed, her voice barely above a whisper. The scent of her hair—vanilla and fresh hay—was intoxicating. His heart hammered against his chest, each beat a drumline to the tension that crackled in the air.

"Any time," he replied, his hands lingering at her sides for a moment longer than necessary.

Their gazes locked. Her lips parted slightly, an invitation he felt powerless to decline. With deliberate slowness, he leaned in, his breath mingling with hers, until there was no space left for doubts or second thoughts.

Her lips met his in a kiss that was anything but tentative. It was passionate, intense—a conflagration of emotions that had been simmering beneath the surface of their every interaction. The taste of her was sweet, like the sugared rim of a cocktail glass, a hint of mischief wrapped in allure.

Dolly responded with equal fervor, her fingers threading through his hair, pulling him closer. Their bodies pressed together, her curves melding into his angles, as if they were two puzzle pieces finally fitting into place. The softness of her mouth against his rugged one was a contrast that sent a shudder through him.

Nash savored the feeling of her against him, the way her chest rose and fell in quick succession, mirroring his own erratic breathing. The sensation of her heartbeat pounding through the thin fabric of her shirt created a rhythm that danced in tandem with his.

For a stolen moment, nothing else existed outside the cocoon of their embrace—the looming threat of Jackson Blevins's illicit activities, the expectations of a life lived in the narrow confines of right and wrong—all faded into insignificance. In the dim light of the horse barn, Nash felt Dolly's pulse quicken as his hands steadied her waist. Their breath mingled, a silent conversation of desire that no words could convey.

"And I thought I was going to catch a couple of horse thieves." Finn's voice cut through the thick air of the barn, abrupt and unwelcome. Shadows shifted as he stepped into view from around a stall, a half-eaten apple in his hand revealing his unannounced presence. He pulled on a chain and harsh overhead lights flashed on.

Dolly drew back, her cheeks red. She smoothed down her shirt, in an attempt to restore some semblance of order after their heated embrace. Her eyes darted between Nash and Finn.

"Evening, Finn," Nash said, tamping down on his annoyance. He ran a hand through his hair, trying to feign indifference. The taste of Dolly's lips lingered, a bittersweet reminder of what they had just jeopardized.

"Didn't mean to interrupt," Finn replied, crunching into his apple with a casualness that belied the tension now threading the air. He leaned against the wooden frame of the stall, a silent observer to the undercurrents swirling between them. "But I wanted to make my presence known before things went any further."

Dolly flushed deep crimson.

"I wasn't aware that someone has been stealing horses," Nash said, stepping in front of her protectively.

"Not stealing, yet. But definitely messing around with equipment. Stardust's food was knocked on the floor. Beatrice's bridle was on the floor of the stable, half covered in horseshit. And the barn door was left unlocked on more than one occasion."

"Did you report this to security?" Nash asked.

Finn shook his head. "I figured we'd handle it ourselves. Probably just dumb kids or someone who would see the error in their ways with a good beatdown."

"Probably," Nash said.

Dolly bit her lip, and uncharacteristically, hid behind him. Nash watched her closely, noted the subtle shift in her posture, the way her hands clenched ever so slightly at her sides. She seemed to be afraid of something. Could she suspect Finn was working with Blevins?

"What are you two doing out here so late? Loretta kick you out of the RV?" Finn grinned.

"No," Dolly said, clearing her throat.

"Because she and Taylor have been getting kind of close."

"Nash and I were just…walking," she said lamely.

This was going to be more fuel for the rumor mill, but he might as well roll with it.

"Is that what the kids are calling it these days?" Finn said.

"It's my fault," Nash said. "I had wanted to take a look at the bulls. I was wondering if the Mexican fighting bulls had arrived for tomorrow's lineup or if we would have to wait until Laredo."

"Nah, we won't see them until the next rodeo."

"I wonder if they're really as tough as they say."

"Me too." Finn's interest was piqued. His apple was forgotten as he tossed it aside. "I don't know much about them, but usually the Mexican fighting bulls are more squirrely than other breeds. I do know Blevins is particular about his stock."

"Particular, how?" Dolly asked.

"He doesn't let anyone handle the bulls but his own guys," Finn said. "Says they're too temperamental for the average Joe."

"Which guys?"

"Hector, Taylor, and Ryan."

Bingo. Nash tried to conceal his excitement.

"Taylor Keating?" Dolly said faintly.

"Yeah, your sister's sweetie. He's got a way with bulls."

"And bullshit," she muttered.

"Hector Ortiz is from Jaripeo, right? I figured he'd

know his own bulls. But Ryan Chester is originally from Rocky Ridge out of Canada, right?" Nash asked.

Finn scratched his chin. "I don't know. Ryan's been working for the UPRC for as long as I've been here. I don't really know him or Hector all that well. Maybe we could ask them for tips on riding those devils."

"Good idea," Nash said.

"Anyway, I'm sorry I interrupted you guys. I could come back in a half hour. Would that give you two enough time?"

Dolly exhaled a shuddering breath. "We should go," she muttered, her words as unsteady as her steps as she nearly ran out of the barn. That wasn't like the Dolly he had come to know. She didn't get embarrassed easily, at least he didn't think so. Besides, it was just a kiss. They hadn't gotten *that* carried away. He shrugged at Finn, who tugged on the string to return the barn to darkness.

"Are you all right?" Nash said, hurrying to catch up with Dolly.

"Fine. Just fine."

"I'm sure Finn's not going to say anything."

She gave a bitter laugh. "Of course he is. Bull riders gossip worse than old ladies. But that's okay. I'm sure Pat has already gotten the ball rolling on that news."

"Well, at least Finn didn't think we were snooping around."

"No, he thought we were screwing around."

"Well," Nash said. "To be fair. We were."

He should be focusing on Jackson Blevins. Instead, his mind replayed the softness of Dolly's lips, the desperate grip of her fingers, and the way her body had pressed against his—no, this was not the time for distractions. "Look, maybe I was out of line with the kiss…" he began.

She whirled on him. "No, that's not it. I liked it. The kiss."

He was pleasantly surprised. "Then why are you running like your tail's on fire?"

Folding her arms in front of her, Dolly bit her lip. "I just don't like an audience."

"Are you sure that's all that's bothering you?" he asked, stroking his fingers down her cheek.

"I guess I'm just tired. It's been a long day. And tomorrow is gearing up to be a longer one."

That was true. They walked back to her Winnebago in silence.

"Do you think the coast is clear?" he asked.

"It better be. If it's not, expect to see Taylor running out of there in a few minutes with his underwear on and carrying his boots."

"I could come inside with you," he asked, wondering if he sounded hopeful or desperate.

"Tempting. But I'll see you tomorrow."

"See you," he said. At least the night had given him some new leads to follow. And one hell of a kiss.

Chapter Ten

Dolly

DAY TWO OF opening weekend was going strong. If all their rodeos this year were this well attended, it would go a long way to easing the pressure off her to try and get their social media posts to go viral. She was trying to find the courage to leave her home office in the Winnebago and get some more footage of the rodeo. She really should be concentrating on the other athletes in the UPRC, but she was itching to get back into the investigation.

The image of Finn catching her kissing Nash last night played on repeat in her mind like a cruel slideshow. If he told his father... God, Jefferson might remember her from her escort days, and then all hell would break loose. Her stomach churned at the thought. Maybe she should reach out to Jefferson herself, plead her case before Finn spilled the beans. With a decisive click, she looked up his number and saved it, just in case.

Dragging her thoughts away from the dangerous precipice of her past, she turned her attention to the work piled up on her virtual desk. Photos from the shoot with Nash and Donnan still needed editing. As she clicked through the raw images, a smile tugged at her lips. Donnan was undeniably adorable, but Nash... Oh boy, he looked downright sexy in those cowboy boots and tight jeans. Her mind wandered to that stolen kiss, the heat of his body pressed against hers...and Finn clicking on the light in the barn.

Blevins texted her. *Stop spending time on losers. I fired all the non-performers. They won't be back. I want to see some posts on our top athletes in all events.*

"Jerk," she ground out.

She texted back: *What about Nash Weaver? Didn't you see the buzz he's getting with Donnan?*

No one cares about the baby cow. They want action. They want T&A. What's your sister LeAnn's number? I think she blocked me.

She was not going to answer that question. If Blevins asked for a T&A shot from LeAnn, being blocked was probably the safest course before Dylan got wind of that nonsense. She screen-shot the conversation for the record anyway, but then she switched off her phone. She needed a break from Blevins. She powered down her computer and put it aside. It was almost time to go meet Nash at the gate anyway.

On her way, she passed by Reba who was in her veterinarian's golf cart. Reba swung around to pick her up.

"What's this I hear about you banging Nash in the barn last night?" Reba asked as she climbed in.

"It was one kiss." Leave it to the rumor mill to blow things out of proportion.

"Uh-huh. Pat tells me you and Nash looked really cozy..." Reba glared at her. "I hope you're not messing around in Nash's investigation."

"I'm helping."

Reba snorted. "He doesn't need your help with that."

Dolly wasn't so sure about that. "Just between you and me, he told me that Victor Lance knows something about Blevins but is too afraid to say anything."

"What do you think he knows?" Reba frowned.

"The question is why is he covering it up?"

"Yeah, especially since Vanessa is trying to get him charged with murder. She won't get it, but it might be manslaughter."

"Do you think you could talk to Dr. Lance?" Dolly asked.

"Me? No. I don't think I could control my temper. He could have killed LeAnn. And if Shane found out I was talking with the man who drugged Sverre, he'd be pissed that I didn't ask him to come along. And I'd never ask him to talk to Victor, because then I'd need bail money."

"Yeah, I see that." It was discouraging news, but nothing that she hadn't expected.

"Just be careful around Nash," Reba said. "He's only going to be around until he solves the case. This is just a fun fling for you, right?"

"There's nothing between us," she said. But she was pretty sure she was lying to Reba, and she was pretty sure Reba knew that as well. "Has Loretta sold anything today?" Dolly said, changing the subject.

"I haven't been able to get away to see how she's doing."

"I'll go." Dolly hesitated. "How well do you know Taylor Keating?"

Reba shrugged. "He's a nice guy."

"Is he?" Dolly wanted desperately to believe that.

"I think so. His father is great. And they've got a close relationship." Reba fixed her with a stern look. "Don't go mother-henning Loretta. She doesn't need you to butt in on her life just because you're roommates."

"Anyone ever tell you that you're a hypocrite?" Dolly crossed her arms over her chest.

"No one who wanted to live." Reba reached down and grabbed some dirty hay from a bucket in the back.

"Don't you dare," Dolly shrieked, and hopped out of the slow-moving golf cart before Reba could even think about throwing the hay at her. Reba could give unsolicited advice to her about Nash, but it wasn't okay for Dolly to be concerned about Loretta's romance? That didn't seem fair.

Dolly stalked over to where the vendors were gearing up for another busy day. The handcrafts section wasn't that busy yet, so she was able to sit next to Loretta as she worked on a watercolor painting of Donnan.

"How's it going?"

"Good," Loretta said, swirling her brush into a honey-brown color.

"Sell anything?"

"A few paintings yesterday. A couple of kits. I'm not going to be rich anytime soon, but I'm paying the bills."

"Good." Dolly wasn't sure how to broach the subject. Luckily, Loretta beat her to it.

"Taylor and I are just having fun."

"It's none of my business," Dolly said.

"When has that ever stopped anyone in this family?"

That was true. "Does he work with Jackson Blevins directly?" Dolly asked.

"As much as you do, I guess."

Huh, that didn't answer any of her burning questions. Dolly tried another tactic. "I hear that he's going to be handling the new shipment of Mexican bulls that are coming to Laredo next week."

"That's his job." Loretta shrugged. "Bullfighting, bull riding and bull handling."

"As long as he's not bullshitting."

"Yeah." Loretta gave a half laugh, but concentrated on mixing colors on her palette.

"What does he think of Blevins?"

"We haven't talked about it. Why?"

"I was just wondering."

"You were wondering if he was working with Blevins doing something illegal."

"Shh," Dolly said. She wasn't surprised that Loretta knew. She figured Reba had filled her in. "You can't say anything like that aloud. You could ruin everything."

Loretta gestured with her paintbrush. "There is no one around."

"Still, you can't be too careful."

"Here's what I know. Taylor loves bulls. He sometimes rides them. He sometimes takes care of them. Most of the time, he's in the arena keeping the bull riders safe. When it's over, he either hangs with his father, with his friends, or lately with me. If there's something weird going on, I haven't seen it."

That was some bit of relief.

"And he's a good kisser."

Dolly could have lived without that little bit of information. "Yeah, I saw."

Loretta didn't even look up from her painting. "But I'll keep my eyes open. I don't want to be fooled again."

Dolly felt like a jerk. "I'm sorry. I don't think he's trying to deceive you. I just don't know him."

"And I'm not the best judge of character," Loretta said, giving her an annoyed look over her shoulder.

"I didn't say that."

"You didn't have to. My track record speaks for itself."

Damn her sister's exes. Dolly hoped karma would bite them both on the ass for hurting Loretta. "Those guys were assholes. They were just good at hiding it. That's on them. Not on you."

"Maybe Taylor is an asshole who is good at hiding it too."

"And maybe he's not," Dolly said softly, squeezing Loretta's shoulder in sympathy.

Loretta took in a shaky breath. "I hope not. I really like him."

Dolly didn't feel any better when she left her sister, so she made it a point to promo her stall on all the social media feeds. "Hashtag brilliant artist" and "must buy." She didn't know if it would drive sales, but it couldn't hurt.

Her next stop was the will-call booth. She was about to turn her phone back on, but she saw Nash coming up from the parking lot.

"I need the VIP pass for Nash Weaver," she said to the

person manning the booth.

"Sorry, Dolly. He's been removed from the VIP list."

"By who?" Dolly frowned.

"Mr. Blevins called in a bunch of people. He said they would try and sneak in the rodeo via the VIP system, so he put a stop to it."

Of course, by that time Nash was in earshot. "No problem." He got into the ticket line instead.

"Wait," Dolly said. "I can fix this. There's been a mistake. Nash Weaver is one of my models."

The will-call operator frowned at his list. "I don't want to get into trouble."

Dolly fumbled with her phone. She turned it on. She would text Blevins or Shelby and make this go away. But even before her phone came back on line, Nash reached the beginning of the ticket line.

"One please," Nash said.

"I've got this," Dolly said, wanting to shake her phone, as if that would make it go faster.

"Thanks," Nash said, taking his ticket from the other worker. He walked through the gate and into the rodeo.

Exasperated, Dolly hurried over to him. "I'm so sorry about that. Blevins has never done that before."

Nash shrugged. "Doesn't matter."

"I could have gotten you in."

"I'll expense the cost of the ticket back to Shelby, if that's what you're worried about."

"It's not the money. It's the principle of the thing. He shouldn't be sticking his nose into my business."

"He shouldn't be doing a lot of things, but that's why

I'm here." Nash gave her a reassuring smile.

The smile knocked her off-kilter and brought up memories of last night's kiss in her mind. "Are you feeling all right? I figured you'd be all hopped up about this."

"It's just a roadblock to my investigation. To be honest, I'm happy that I don't have to pretend to be a bull rider. It's tough being booed."

"No, I mean not being a VIP. I could have gotten you the pass."

"Why do I need the pass when I have you?"

He had a point.

"Sometimes it's easier to just follow the rules," he said, showing her his ticket.

She resisted the urge to cross her eyes at him. "I was following the rules. Blevins changed them on the fly."

"He does that a lot, I've noticed," Nash said.

"Yeah," Dolly agreed. "Well, I'll fix this for Laredo, don't you worry."

"I'm not worried and neither should you. You know what, I want to hold off on the promos for a few hours."

"Of course you do." Dolly scowled at him.

"Hear me out. When was the last time you took a lunch hour?"

"What does that have to do with anything?"

"Call it more rule following. You're entitled to a break for lunch every day. Do you take it?"

"I eat lunch," Dolly hedged.

Nash just looked at her.

"Usually on the run or while I'm editing on my computer."

He nodded as if he was satisfied. "Good. You and I are going to have a nice lunch around the rodeo. We're not going to talk about Blevins and you're not going to take a picture of your damned hot dog."

"Who are you and what have you done with Nash Weaver?"

"Nash Weaver, bull rider, is gone." He held out his hand to her. "I'm Nash Weaver, private eye."

She took his hand and shook it. The rough calluses on his palms from the bull rope made her shiver when she thought how it would feel on her more intimate areas. "What's that supposed to mean?"

"It means that last night was a turning point for me."

"You mean in terms of the investigation?"

"I mean in terms of us."

"Us." She stopped dead in her tracks and looked up at him.

"I want you. And based on how you kissed me back, you want me too."

She didn't know if she was going to spontaneously combust or melt into the pavement. His honesty and frank assessment were both off-putting and on-turning. "Okay," she said, licking her suddenly dry lips. "What are we going to do about that?"

"We're going to talk." He reached down and grabbed her hand.

"Talk?" she said, a little disappointed. She was hoping for more kisses and cuddles. But she took his hand and went with him to get in line for some walking tacos.

They took their impromptu picnic under one of the

several pavilions that were set up with long tables and bench seating. Giant fans were set up near the tent's ceilings and a water mister was at the front and back end.

"Going to be a hot one," he said as they sat down. It was still early so this area wasn't as packed as it normally would be.

"So what do you want to talk about?" She shifted uncomfortably as she poked into her Frito chili pie with a plastic fork. She wasn't ready to bring up the subject of the cheerleader uniform last night and she was hoping he wasn't going to confront her about Leisure Industries. She wanted to see how serious Nash was about this "us" business. She could lose her job if word got out. And she wasn't fighting this hard to keep this rodeo afloat so she could be kicked out because of the morality clause in her contract.

Did Nash just want a quick lay and a casual fling? If so, she'd be on board with that, but she wasn't about to share her heart or her secrets with him.

Or was he in for the long haul? Dolly wasn't sure they'd be so good together after they got the hot sex they'd been building toward all year out of the way. They were too different. She liked to play hard and fast with the rules and he was the king of rules. But it could be fun while it lasted.

"You never did tell me what had upset you so much last night. That gift that someone dropped off."

Yeah, and she wasn't about to tell him now, either. "Oh that..." She gave an artful laugh. "That was just a misunderstanding. It turned out to be something for

Loretta. An art book." The lie came easily to her. "I thought it was porn."

"Uh-huh," Nash said.

Jeez, he didn't look like he believed her. Was she losing her touch or was he beginning to see through her bullshit? Neither was good. Truth was, she was scared of what that cheerleading outfit meant. At the most benign, someone was being an asshole. But Dolly thought that it was more along the lines of something more nefarious. Blackmail? What on earth would she do then? She didn't have any money to pay off a blackmailer. She'd have to come clean to Nash. Maybe his FBI buddies could help her then. It was just that Nash saw the world in black and white, with no room for gray. Her past was gray, and could very well come back to bite her in the ass at any minute.

She polished off her meal and sprang up to dump the wrapper in the trash. See, this is why she was a workaholic. She didn't have to think about serious shit like this when she was taking pictures and working as a spin doctor.

"You okay?" Nash said coming up behind her. His hands felt solid and comforting on her shoulders.

"I'm still rattled about Blevins firing you and stepping over my request at the will-call booth. I think it would be best if we just headed down to the Rocky Ridge Ranch's pavilion and get in some Donnan time. I can distract the workers with a behind-the-scenes interview while you check out his area."

"Honestly, I think if there was something to find, we missed it. The next rodeo in Laredo is the key event to do a search and investigation. The bulls from Jaripeo Ranch are coming up from Mexico and if Rocky Ridge has something in a secret compartment, they'll move it on the first day in Laredo."

Dolly blew out a frustrated breath. "Okay, I guess I don't have to promo you this weekend. Let Blevins forget about you. Well, now what?"

"Now, you need to stop working so hard." Nash gently turned her around. "It's not worth it until Shelby is rid of Blevins. I don't want to alarm you," he said. "But this season might be the UPRC's last, if Blevins keeps up what he's been doing."

Dolly pushed down that familiar anxiety. She was no longer a scared twenty-something kid out of a job. She could always live in the Winnebago, if she lost her apartment. She could always mooch off of LeAnn or Reba, if she didn't want to go back home. She had options.

Being jobless didn't equate to being homeless anymore and it sure didn't mean she'd have to consider something like escorting again. She could freelance her PR skills. She could...

"Are you all right?" Nash said.

Dolly forced herself to take a slow drink of her iced tea before answering him. "I'm fine."

"You look like you're about to cry."

Did she?

She blew out a shaky breath. "I know that attendance is down. It doesn't help that we've had more tragedy than a Shakespearean play lately. Ronnie Sunderland's death, two crazed bulls, and don't even get me started on the doping and gambling scandal. Seems like Blevins might be driving this rodeo into the ground on purpose. We need to find that evidence against Blevins before he puts the final nail in the UPRC coffin." She really loved her job and she didn't want to start over. But more importantly, she didn't think she *could* start over again.

"Me. Not we."

"We're in this together, buddy. Whether you like it or not."

"Why?" he asked.

Dolly realized that she was white-knuckled and forced herself to unclench her fists. "This job is important to me."

"It's important to Shelby, too."

She was pretty sure that Shelby would land on her feet if the company went under. Dolly wasn't so sure about herself. "After I was let go from the football club, I tried a lot of things. And I failed at a lot of things."

She met his gaze. Nash's eyes were warm and sympathetic. She wondered if they would turn scornful and hateful if she went into details. She didn't want to take a risk like that right now. "I wanted to be a YouTuber or an influencer. But I couldn't get enough likes and followers to make the ads profitable. I really had to struggle."

"And you're worried that if you lose your job, you'd go back to struggling?"

That hit a little too close to home for her to deal with just now. "Do we have to talk about this, right now? I thought we were going to get away from Blevins for a bit."

"Sorry," he said. "You're right. I'm breaking my own rules. It's a hard habit to get out of, switching from business to pleasure."

"I think I'd like to concentrate on the pleasure part of it."

She was rewarded with that sexy grin again.

"You're going to be all right," he said, and stood up. He pulled her to her feet and brushed a kiss over her forehead.

Dolly's breath caught. Time seemed to stop. She could put her hand on his shoulder and stop him from moving away. She wanted more. It would be so nice to lose herself in a kiss and see where it led. But did she want to start something without knowing how he was going to react if he found out she'd been an escort?

"How do you know?" The words were hard to force out, but she was getting lost in his intense gaze.

"Because I won't let anything happen to you or to Shelby."

She lifted her hand and touched his cheek. He closed his eyes and leaned into it with a soft smile on his face. "Let's take the day and spend some time together."

"It's the second day of the season," she choked out. "I can't take the day off."

"If I know you, you've already scheduled your posts for today."

She had. But she had also wanted to do some live action shots.

"And I can cover for you with Shelby."

Dolly put a hand over her heart. "Nash Weaver, you'd lie?"

"See what a bad influence you are on me?"

"No, but I'd like to."

"Well then," he said. "Why don't we head out to my motel?"

"I've got a better idea. Let's hit the Winnebago. That way if something does require my attention, we're right on site."

"I admire your dedication," he said.

"Is that all you admire about me?"

"Not by a long shot."

The day was looking up. And with Loretta busy in vendor row selling her paintings, Dolly was looking forward to having a few hours to make some of the fantasies she'd been entertaining over the last year about Nash come true.

Chapter Eleven

Dolly

"IT FEELS A little like playing hooky," Dolly said as she opened up the Winnebago's door. Nash stepped in, looking enormous in the small space. She locked the door and turned the air conditioner a notch higher. They were going to need it. "Can I get you a drink?"

"All I need is you," he said.

Well, all right then. Kicking off her shoes, she walked into Nash's arms. Unable to resist, she tilted her head up and gave in to every thought she'd had since the kiss last night. She captured his lips with her own, initiating a kiss that was filled with desperation and urgency.

Nash responded eagerly, his tongue teasing hers, exploring her mouth with a possessive hunger that left her breathless. His lips were soft and warm under hers. When Nash deepened the kiss, the intensity of it made her head spin. She gave herself up to the feelings that she had been dreaming about. His mouth was hot and his kisses long and sensual. He stroked her back. That felt nice. Real nice. She cuddled in closer to him, the tips of her hardened nipples brushing against the hard planes of his chest.

Pressed against him, she thrilled at the growing hardness she felt beneath his jeans. She broke away, her eyes wide and flushed with desire. Nash's face was just as flushed, his cheeks reddened under the glinting shine of sweat. She unbuttoned her blouse, her fingers clumsy. She nearly swallowed her tongue when he stripped off his shirt and tossed it to the floor. She had a moment to admire strong abs and a tight chest before he helped her with her blouse and then her bra.

Their breathing was heavy and fast, their differences, the investigation, completely irrelevant at the moment. All that mattered now was the heat between them, burning brighter and stronger with every passing second.

"I've been dreaming of this for the past year." He traced his fingers over her breasts, pebbling her nipples almost painfully. He leaned down and kissed the tops of them while his strong hands stroked and caressed her sensitive skin. It sent shivers down her spine.

"Me too," she gasped out.

Feeling bold, Dolly reached for the waistband of Nash's pants, unzipping them with trembling fingers. She wrapped her hand around his cock, delighting in the way he tensed and gritted his teeth at her touch.

Nash closed his eyes and groaned as she rubbed him up and down.

The sound of their breathing filled the small space, mingling with the scent of his aftershave. Dolly could feel the heat emanating from Nash's body, a steady warmth that both comforted and excited her.

Nash's lips found her neck, his teeth nibbling at her

delicate skin. She shivered involuntarily, her breath hitching as his hand cupped her breasts.

"N-Nash…" she murmured softly, the word catching in her throat as he continued to explore her, his touch pure magic.

His thumb trailed around her nipple, circling it gently. She arched into his touch. He took her nipple into his mouth, sending waves of pleasure coursing through her. She stroked him harder, her mind filled with fantasies of what it would feel like to have him inside her. The thought only fueled her arousal, intensifying the ache between her thighs. Nash pushed up her skirt and slid his hand down her panties.

She was soaking wet and trembling on his flickering fingers. Dolly bit her lip, barely suppressing a moan as Nash's fingers slowly drove her wild with pleasure. The sensation of his skilled fingers dancing over her wet folds was intoxicating, sending shudders of pleasure through her body. Her hand felt clumsy on his thick cock as she continued to pump him with her fist.

"I like your touch," he growled.

As Nash gently pushed one finger inside her, Dolly's breath hitched. The pressure built within her, the mounting pleasure becoming almost unbearable. Her nails dug into his shoulders, her grip tightening as he added another finger, stretching and filling her in the most delicious way.

Dolly let out a shaking whimper as Nash's thumb circled her throbbing clit, sending shockwaves of pleasure throughout her entire body. Her hips bucked against his hand, silently pleading for more. She moaned softly, her breath catching in her throat as he continued to explore her. With each touch, Dolly became dizzier with desire and need. She knew she had to have him, to feel his cock inside her, to let him take control and give her the release she so desperately craved.

"Come for me," Nash whispered, his voice a husky reminder that only heightened the thrill of their illicit encounter. With each stroke, Dolly edged closer to orgasm. Their eyes locked, communicating more than words ever could, as they shared this intensely intimate moment.

Just as Dolly felt herself teetering on the edge of an earth-shattering climax, Nash said, "Tell me what you want, sweetheart." Nash's voice was low and seductive. "Tell me how much you need me."

"God, Nash," she murmured into his lips, her voice breathy and laced with desire. "I want you so much it hurts."

"Then let me take away the pain," he growled, his large palm cradling the back of her neck, keeping her anchored to him as he fingered her to an explosive orgasm. Her hand opened up in shock, letting his hard cock go. She went up on her toes, her head flung back as she rode the waves of pleasure. He stoked her slower now, her body twitching as she gasped with each tender flick of his fingers.

"I want you inside me. I need you to fuck me."

They stripped off the rest of their clothes.

"Condom," he said, bending down to grab one from his pocket and slid it on.

Without another wasted moment, Nash hoisted Dolly up. Her legs wrapped around his waist as he pinned her against the door of the Winnebago. She gasped as Nash thrust into her, filling her completely in one swift motion. Heat and need roared through Dolly's veins as she melted into him. She twined her arms around his neck, fingers sinking into his hair. This was real. Raw and the sweetest thing she'd ever known.

She lost herself in the pleasure he bestowed upon her, relishing in the feeling of him deep inside her. Every touch was like a spark igniting a wildfire within her, making it impossible for her to resist him any longer.

In that moment, there was no past or future—only this overwhelming present where she and Nash shared a connection that was almost magical. She didn't want to think about what would come after this. She only wanted to savor every blissful moment. Their movements were desperate and frenzied, driven by pure lust and insatiable hunger.

Dolly clung to Nash as he drove into her, each powerful stroke bringing her closer and closer to the edge. Her breath came in ragged gasps, her nails digging into his back as she braced herself for the impending release. As if sensing her nearness, Nash quickened his pace, his movements becoming more forceful and deliberate.

Their bodies moved together in perfect sync, each touch and kiss eliciting moans and gasps from both of them. Dolly lost herself in the sensations, drowning out the voice of reason in favor of following the wild desires coursing through her body.

Finally, Dolly could no longer contain herself, and she surrendered to the pleasure coursing through her veins. Her orgasm ripped through her like a tidal wave, leaving her trembling and breathless. Nash followed soon after, his own climax racking his body with shudders of ecstasy.

As the aftershocks subsided, Dolly and Nash exchanged a tender, lingering kiss. As the last shudders of pleasure waned, Dolly and Nash reluctantly pulled apart, their bodies slick with sweat and desire.

"Holy hell, that was wild," Dolly said.

"Yeah," he agreed, pushing the hair out of his face. "Now let's hit the bed and take our time."

Dolly's knees went wobbly.

SEVERAL HOURS LATER, Dolly was feeling better about the whole Blevins and the UPRC situation. She'd figure out something before things got too bad. And she had Nash working full-time on his investigation. She'd make sure that Shelby personally got Nash into Laredo as a VIP and, together, they would check out the Rocky Ridge storage area and the Jaripeo storage area. Unfortunately, that still left one suspect: Taylor Keating. As she was thinking about it, her phone buzzed on the small night table.

Reaching over, she saw a text from Finn. *Meet me in the VIP area.*

What the hell? Bull riders didn't send her texts like that.

Why? she texted back.

He sent back emojis of cheerleaders.

Dolly flashed hot and then cold. She started to shake.

Finn had sent the uniform. And the nasty *"How much?"* card that had gone with it. The only question now was what was he going to do with that knowledge? Had it been a sick joke? Or something more sinister?

She pushed back the covers and took a quick shower. Thoughts flew around in her head. How was she going to spin this? What damage control could she do? She was still shaking when she got dressed in jeans and a T-shirt. After she laced on her sneakers, she turned to Nash who was dozing with one muscular arm over his eyes. She didn't have to do this alone. But she wasn't sure how to bring him in on this. She wanted him for backup, but she didn't want him to be broadsided by the information about her past. Biting her lip, she considered just leaving him here.

"Nash?" Dolly nudged him.

"Hmm?"

"I need you to meet me by the bull-riding arena." She'd get there first. Find out what Finn wanted and do damage control. By the time Nash got there, it would be all over or he'd be charging in like a white knight.

"What? Why?" he said grouchily. "I don't have to do promos there anymore."

"Thanks for reminding me. We still need you to do some work with Donnan." Donnan was the last thing on her mind at the moment, but she was glad to use him as an excuse.

Nash groaned and rolled over with the pillow over his head.

"We have a week until Laredo to get a series with you and that cute little calf all over social media. If we make you famous, no one is going to look twice at you being backstage at the rodeo."

"Where are you going?" he asked, rolling back over.

"I told you, the bull-riding event. The last show is at three p.m."

"Why do I have to be there?"

Yeah, that was a good question. She racked her brain and came up with the perfect excuse on the fly. Dolly unplugged her phone from the charger. "I know Shane and the Viking Ranch are innocent. I'm hoping Taylor Keating is too. I want to get Taylor out of the way today so you and I can concentrate on the other two ranches in Laredo."

"Wait," he said, sitting up.

"Just meet me there. I'll set up the promos so it won't look suspicious that we're questioning Taylor."

"Dolly," he started to say, blinking confusedly at her.

But she was already out the door. Should she have told him everything and waited for him to go with her? Probably. But there was still a chance she could salvage the situation without revealing her past. If she didn't have to, she didn't want to ruin this perfect afternoon with Nash. If things went to hell in the next couple of days, well then at least she'd have one pleasant memory of today to look back on.

But she really hoped it didn't. For the first time in a long while, Dolly wondered what it would be like to be in a relationship again. Of course, she would have to let Nash in on her secret past. But that was getting ahead of herself. One day at a time. One week to Laredo. If they were able to pin something on Blevins, then her job was safe and she would feel more secure in her life and be able to tell Nash everything. In theory.

Pushing that aside, she headed back into the rodeo grounds from her employee spot and made a beeline to the bull-riding area.

"Hey, Dolly," Finn said, coming up to her.

She tensed. Looking around, she realized that they were relatively alone. Was this when he would reveal that he sent her the uniform and that obnoxious note?

"Hey, Finn." Dolly feigned nonchalance, but she scanned the area looking for exit routes and people she could shout to for help if she needed to. "So what's with the cheerleaders?"

"Mr. Blevins wants you to do some reels with me."

"He does?" Dolly checked her phone, but there wasn't anything from Blevins specifically about that today. But that didn't mean anything. He had a tendency to assume she could read his mind.

"Yeah. Come on back to the VIP area."

Here it comes, Dolly thought. She followed him, fumbling with her phone to turn on her voice recording app. She toggled it on. If Finn thought he was going to blackmail her or proposition her, she was going to get it on tape and then take it straight to Shelby Miller. Shelby had supported Reba last year when Reba told her about the awful experience she'd had with her old boss. Dolly knew Shelby would be an ally if things shook down wrong.

Rounding the corner, though, Dolly stopped dead in her tracks. Two beautiful women in generic cheerleading outfits were posing by a mechanical bull and a saddle.

"Okay," Finn said to Dolly. "Where do you want me?"

All right. Not what she had been expecting. Relief made her knees weak. It looked like this was a legitimate photo shoot. Dolly sat on a hay bale while she got herself together.

The cheerleaders were too coincidental coming on the heels of her getting the uniform. Or were they? Dolly couldn't rule out that she was being oversensitive.

"Everything all right?"

"Yeah," she said, swallowing hard. "Just taking a moment to picture the story I want to tell."

"Righteous," he said, and went over to chat up one of the models.

Dolly knew she needed to get off her ass and get started, but she was having a hard time breathing now that she was coming down from the stress of the fight-or-flight adrenaline she had just put herself through.

Do your job, she told herself.

"All right." Dolly stood up. She wished Blevins had scheduled this with her previously. She would have brought a better camera than her cell phone. But this would work in a pinch. First he overrode her at the VIP booth and now this. She was going to have to meet with him on Monday in the Dallas office and address this. She'd take Shelby with her for safety. Blevins didn't get to do this to her.

Dolly shut off her recorder and had Finn pose with the models for a few shots. Then because she was feeling ornery, she had Finn take off his shirt and give it to one of the women and then she shot cheesecake pictures of him. To his credit, Finn didn't seem to mind, and it wound up being a productive shoot. She'd be able to use the footage in several videos.

"Let's do this on a real bull," Finn said.

"Not with them dressed like that," Dolly said. "They could get hurt. If you want them in the ring with a bull, we're going to have to find a tamer one, and no one gets on his back."

Finn pouted, but the models looked relieved.

Dolly called Shane. He said he didn't have a bull that fit the bill here in Killeen, but he could send a bull named Ferdinand to Laredo next week. After checking with the models' schedules—they were free next Saturday—she booked them for a few hours at the Laredo rodeo. She'd have enough time to write a "We're cowgirls, of course we..." script for them to say for one of the sessions.

"Thanks," Finn said as they left the VIP area. "That was fun."

Yeah, it had been. Now that they were alone, she waited for him to mention something about the cheerleader uniform, but he didn't. He seemed more concerned about looking pretty for his bull ride that was coming up. She left him to his primping and headed to the chute area where they were loading in the bulls.

If it hadn't been Finn who sent the cheerleader outfit, who had it been? She was filming the bulls in their pens when Nash came running in.

"Everything okay?" he asked.

"It is now," she said. And without caring who was watching, she launched herself into his arms and gave him a huge kiss.

Chapter Twelve

Dolly

"WELL, THAT'S A consolation prize," Finn drawled. "For getting kicked off the roster."

Dolly reluctantly broke off the kiss, but when she tried to move away, Nash held her close to his side. "Yeah, it is," he said.

"Which bull did you choose?" she asked Finn, refusing to be embarrassed.

"Windbreaker."

Dolly blinked. "Seriously."

"I think they were going for a Tornado feel, rather than…"

"Windbreaker the farting bull?"

He gave her a grim nod.

"You better stay on him," Dolly said.

"I plan to." Finn adjusted his gear as he prepared for his ride.

"I hope so." Dolly set her camera up so she could record the eight seconds of action. She didn't want to imagine what the social media trolls would have to say about a failed ride on a bull with that name.

Windbreaker blew him away.

Talk about a gas-tastrophe!

Looks like Finn underestimated Windbreaker's fartistry.

"So, you want to tell me why you rushed out here like your ass was on fire?" Nash asked quietly as they made their way to the VIP spectator section.

"I told you…"

"And you were lying," he said grimly.

Shit. He could see her bullshit.

"And you still don't trust me even after…" He broke off. "I thought things would be different, if we acted on our feelings, but I guess not."

"It's complicated," she said.

"No, it's just easier to keep secrets."

Dolly slowly nodded.

"Does this have anything to do with Blevins?"

"No." She scowled at him. "How can you say that?"

"Maybe I don't trust you either."

Dolly closed her eyes, surprised at how much that hurt. It was worse because she deserved it. "I'm sorry." She should tell him. She should lay it all out on the line and if he judged her for it, then she could just walk away and not have to worry about getting her heart broken.

Instead, she busied herself getting ready for the shot. Work soothed her. She was good at it. This relationship stuff? She sucked at it.

"When I catch Blevins and this is all over, I'm going to leave."

Dolly didn't want him to go.

"Unless you give me a reason to stay."

"I need a little more time."

"Why?"

"Because this isn't easy for me. Trusting men. Relying on someone. Because my livelihood is at stake and I'm scared."

For a moment, Dolly thought Nash would turn away and leave her. It was what she deserved after all. But he surprised her. He had a way of doing that. He rubbed a circle on her back. "Okay. We've waited a year to be together. What's a little longer?"

Her throat tightened and tears threatened. That was crazy in itself. She never cried. "Okay," she whispered.

Then, the gate swung open, and Windbreaker burst out into the arena, kicking up dust and snorting loudly. Dolly eased into work mode and it settled her. Finn's form was tight and controlled as he rode out the first few seconds of the bull's wild bucking. The crowd cheered, urging him on as he countered each of Windbreaker's erratic movements. Windbreaker spun and twisted in an attempt to dislodge Finn from his back. But Finn was unyielding, his focus unwavering even as the bull's movements grew more violent. Windbreaker was a force of nature determined to throw him off. Yet, Finn handled his every move. Dust swirled around them, adding to the electrifying atmosphere of the moment, but really fudging up her shot. She'd have to see about editing that back a bit.

As Windbreaker made one final attempt to unseat Finn with a powerful buck, Finn leaned into the motion, his body fluid and responsive. Finn not only stayed on, but managed to ride out the full eight seconds.

The buzzer sounded, signaling Finn's successful ride. He hopped off and greeted the crowd with a wave of his hat. But then the bull pivoted and charged as Finn's back was turned.

"Look out!" Dolly screamed along with a hundred other people.

The bullfighters dove in, trying desperately to distract Windbreaker. Dolly saw Taylor Keating sprinting toward Finn and the oncoming beast. Taylor leaped in front of Finn, waving his arms wildly and shouting at the top of his lungs to draw the bull's attention away from the bull rider. Dolly struggled to breathe as Windbreaker's massive form bore down on the two men. Taylor grabbed him by the horns and twisted his head.

Finn used the distraction to run for the fence and with the help of Nash and another bull rider, Finn leapt out of harm's way. Taylor dodged and weaved around Windbreaker's aggressive lunges, his movements balletic yet precise. It was as if time had slowed down, each second stretching into an eternity.

"Crap, crap," Dolly said, realizing belatedly that she wasn't getting all of this. She had been distracted. She snapped the camera back up and hoped to be able to splice together a thrilling reel for the fans.

The other bullfighters leaped into action, surrounding Windbreaker and trying to corral him away from Taylor. His movements were a blur of agility and daring, his every step calculated to evade Windbreaker's horns.

Marty Kreeger, the wrangler, galloped in on his horse and tossed a rope on Windbreaker, but missed.

In a split second that felt like an eternity, Taylor made a daring move, sidestepping the bull at the last possible moment. Windbreaker thundered past him, and Marty's second cast got Windbreaker and he was able to hustle the bull toward the exit chute. As the crowd erupted into cheers and applause, a wave of relief washed over Dolly that no one had been hurt.

She pushed her way back to where the cowboys hung around waiting their turn to ride. Finn already had a beer in his hand and his arm around a buckle bunny.

"Are you okay?" Dolly asked, hoping her voice sounded light and not showing the trace of fear. It had been bad enough feeling this way when she watched LeAnn ride. She hadn't been expecting it with Finn.

Finn gave her a nod, a faint smile touching his lips. "I'm fine. Thanks to Taylor."

"Yeah, he did good." Maybe Loretta's heart was safe with him after all. Unless she watched him square off against a two-thousand-pound bull. That might give Loretta a heart attack.

"At least you stayed on," Nash said, putting his arm around Dolly and securing her to his side. It felt good to be held and that Nash still wanted to hold her, even if he knew she was full of shit.

Taylor came back while the rodeo team was setting up for the next rider. "Are you okay?" he asked Finn.

Please let him not be involved in anything, Dolly thought. *For Loretta's sake.*

"Yeah, thanks to you. I appreciate the help out there."

"It's my job," Taylor said.

Dolly wasn't sure what to say. It would be weird if she thanked him too and Taylor was making it a point to not look at her. His ears were tinged with pink too. She bet he was embarrassed that she had caught him and Loretta making out.

"Well, I've got to get prepped for the next ride." Finn clapped a hand on Taylor's shoulder and walked back to the chute area after giving the girl on his arm a kiss and a swat on her ass.

When Taylor went to follow, Nash cleared his throat. "Wait a second, Taylor. Got a question for you. I've been meaning to ask you. I saw you buying something yesterday. What was it?"

"Uh…" Taylor seemed shocked by the question. "It was nothing," Taylor said, trying to brush off Nash's inquiry.

Nash arched an eyebrow, his gaze piercing. "Didn't look like nothing. What was in the bag?"

Taylor shifted uncomfortably, glancing around as if looking for an escape. "It's just something I picked up for Loretta."

Dolly's curiosity piqued. "For Loretta?"

Taylor nodded, his jaw tight. "Yeah, just a little surprise. She said that she liked turquoise and one of the guys said his sister made jewelry down in Mexico and he could get me a good deal." He looked at Dolly for the first time. "I don't make a lot of money, and I wanted to get her something nice. Hector said it wouldn't turn her neck green, so I went for it."

"Hector Ortiz?" Nash said.

"Yeah, you want me to hook you up with him?"

"I'd like that."

"It won't be much of a surprise," Taylor said. "Now that Dolly knows you're going to get budget jewelry."

"It's the thought that counts," Dolly said. "And I'm sure that Loretta is going to love the necklace because it came from you."

"You won't tell her I'm a cheapskate?"

"No. And you're not. You're a smart shopper."

"Yeah, well I've got to get back to work." He jerked his thumb over his shoulder.

"Thanks again," Nash said.

"Yeah, thanks," Dolly echoed and watched him go.

"You want a necklace?" Nash asked her.

Dolly held up her hand. "I'd rather have a flashy ring."

"Well if you want me to put a ring on it, you're going to have to do me a favor."

She narrowed her eyes at him. "I'm not letting you out of your photo op with Donnan. In fact, we're going to go over to the petting zoo right now and interact with the fans."

"Aw shit," Nash said. But he followed her over to the Rocky Ridge area. And for the rest of the night things were back to normal between them. But Dolly quickly realized that normal wasn't what she wanted with Nash anymore.

AFTER THE RODEO closed down, Dolly took some reels of Nash tucking Donnan in with a UPRC blanket.

"Do you want to come back to my motel room and spend the night?" he asked.

"Tempting," she said. "But I've got to be in the Dallas office early tomorrow morning. Loretta and I are going to drive there tonight."

Nash nodded. "I'm going to head over to Laredo in the morning and set up for the weekend's rodeo as much as I can. Mostly, I'll just establish a base and then scout out the local restaurants and bars."

"Loretta and I will be down on Thursday. Can I stay in your motel room then?"

"You bet."

"Are you sure you're still going to want me?" she asked and then could have cursed herself.

"I'm sure," he said, surprising her by not bringing up her lies and secrets.

She kissed him good night, like it would be the last time she kissed him—because it might. This week, she was going to find a way to tell him everything. He deserved to know. They deserved a chance to make this relationship start off on an open and honest note.

Tingles.

Sparks.

And she really wanted to spend the night with him. She broke away reluctantly. "I'll see you next week, cowboy."

"I'll text you if anything comes up. You do the same."

"I'll text you anyway," she said. "Keep up with the social media likes and comment on every response."

"Jesus Christ," he grumbled and walked away.

Dolly was glad Loretta was still out. It gave her some

134

time to gather her thoughts about what she could do to make sure Blevins got kicked out of the UPRC, and what she was going to do if she had to leave this job either because the UPRC went bankrupt or she was forced out because of the morality clause.

Contingency plans and backup plans. That was what would keep her sane right now. And maybe she'd find a clue as to who had sent her the cheerleader uniform as she monitored how the rodeo stars interacted online.

Sitting down at the small desk that doubled as a dining room table, she opened up her laptop and checked all the cowboys' social media posts. Feeling like a cyber stalker, she dug deep into their profiles and their likes and shares. But after an hour, the only thing she could connect with any of them was that they really liked beer and the bull riders were all boasting about the Mexican fighting bulls coming in. Normally, she'd be thrilled that they were actively involved in marketing. But they'd never done this before, and she wasn't sure where they were getting the photographs of the bulls.

Luckily, LeAnn could help her out with that.

She texted her: *Where did you get that picture of El Jefe?*

It took a few minutes, but LeAnn came back with: *From your press packet about the Jaripeo Ranch.*

That set off alarm bells. Dolly hadn't sent out a press packet and when she told LeAnn that, LeAnn forwarded the email she had received.

This didn't come from me, Dolly texted back after she looked at the information.

Well, that will calm Reba down. She was a little pissed off that you hadn't put together something like this for the Viking

Ranch.

Thanks for this. I'll deal with Reba later, Dolly texted back.

The email had come from UPRCMarketing@UPRC.com, which was the rodeo's official marketing email. Dolly almost never used it. She logged onto the account to see all the activity. Someone had sent a group email out to every bull rider, attaching the professional-looking promotional packet for the Jaripeo Ranch and their bulls. That someone hadn't been her. So who had done her job for her and why hadn't they told her about it?

She sent a text to Shelby with a link to the press packet, asking *WTF?*

But when Shelby didn't get back to her right away, Dolly bit the bullet and texted Blevins.

He responded immediately. *We should talk. Come see me tomorrow around ten in my office.*

Shit.

Well, she had planned to do that anyway.

Chapter Thirteen

Jackson Blevins

JACKSON DIDN'T NEED to attend another whiny meeting with stuck-up Shelby and Benny the bummer accountant. Not when he could send his secretary Debbi to take notes in his place. It didn't matter now anyway. He was smuggling in the good stuff through the border and the drugs were cheap and plentiful. Once he established a stable sales connection, the UPRC wouldn't have to worry about money ever again. He might even make enough to buy that little bitch out of her share and then he wouldn't have to deal with her and Benny's whining about the board's reactions and his overspending.

This latest shipment was the purest shit he'd ever sampled. He did another bump of cocaine even though he was still flying high from the line he'd done with his morning coffee and doughnut. He was looking forward to his meeting with Dolly Keller later. He'd been trying to get some alone time with the busty blond bombshell for ages.

He had been overjoyed to hire her for marketing and public relations, and not just because of her great rack. She used to cheer for his favorite pro team. He even bought her a uniform from them and had it delivered to her. Jackson was hoping she'd model it for him and do a few high kicks. He adjusted himself at the thought.

Normally, he wouldn't risk shitting where he ate, even though, he was already nailing Debbi regularly. But he knew Dolly wouldn't say a damned thing. She had a secret. She'd lied on her application. He only found out about it when he hired an escort from Leisure Industries last week. Normally, Jackson didn't have to pay for sex.

But he'd wanted something a little different. And he didn't want all the annoying small talk before and after. So he had asked around and found out that Leisure Industries had a good reputation. The hooker he had hired was a little overpriced, but then again, he got to do what he wanted with her and didn't get any lip. As he was leaving, though, he took a catalog off the broad's coffee table. It was an old one from a few years ago, but Jackson figured it would be good spank material. And who knew, maybe he could get a discount if he chose an older model.

Well, he had been damned surprised to see a familiar face. Unfortunately, she had been fully dressed but the little black number she had been posing in gave him such a kick stand, he immediately had to pay the chick he was with overtime for a blow job so he could drive home in peace.

Smart-mouthed, big tits Dolly Keller had been a prostitute, and shocker—she had never disclosed that on her job application. Here at the UPRC, they had a firm morality clause that he would use as a reason to fire her tight ass if Dolly wasn't nice to him. Real nice to him.

And if she didn't want to cooperate and decided to

make trouble for him, Jackson had a surefire plan to discredit the little slut. He would say that she came on to him and wanted him to be her sugar daddy, and when he nobly refused her wanton advances, she made up false accusations about him.

After all, who was everyone going to believe? The respected CEO of the rodeo or a former cum slut?

Jackson couldn't wait to tell Dolly all about her new duties, which would start with her on her knees in front of him.

When Jackson's office door was kicked open, it disrupted the boner he had been thinking of stroking to take the edge off.

"Get the fuck out of here," he growled as two grubby-looking men stormed in. "I don't need you today."

"Where's our money?"

"For what?" He hadn't needed their services in a while now.

"We've come to collect."

"At least close the fucking door," Jackson snarled, realizing the goons weren't here to earn some extra cash bashing heads for him.

"You're late with your payment."

Jesus Christ. They were working for his supplier over the border. "I don't believe this shit. I've got to have time to sell the product."

"That's not how it works." The bigger of the two goons got in his face.

"You tell Bedier…" Jackson started to say, but the goon slugged him hard in the gut.

It dropped him to his knees. Pain short-circuited everything in his brain and body. He retched up his jelly doughnut and struggled to breathe. He'd kill them for this. He'd kill all of them.

"Half upon order." The big goon followed up with a short kick to his face.

Fireworks exploded behind his eyes. Jackson rocked back, clutching his broken nose.

"And the other half upon delivery." The next kick was to his groin.

Black and red colors hammered into his brain. He couldn't breathe. He was nothing but a streak of misery. He was going to pass out. He was going to die. He tried to speak, but all that came out was a tortured moan. Coiling into a fetal position, Jackson rocked back and forth trying to ease the screaming agony that battered into him with every breath.

"The goods were delivered last week. Where's the money?"

"I'll…" Jackson tried to suck in air. Tried to talk around the blood that was streaming down his throat.

"You'll wire it by this afternoon, or we'll be back. We won't be as agreeable as we are now," the smaller of the two goons said, sweeping a hand across Jackson's desk and knocking everything on the floor. "Do better next time. Or it will be the last shipment you ever get."

"The last shipment you'll be alive to get," the bigger goon clarified. They kicked him a few more times to make sure he got the message.

As Jackson shook on the floor, the two goons rifled

through the rest of his office. They took his personal stash of blow and all the money in his wallet and in his special drawer in his desk.

"This is for our trouble," the smaller man said, fanning the bills out and waving them at Jackson. "It doesn't cover what you owe Bedier."

And then they thankfully left, closing the door behind them.

Needless to say, when Dolly Keller walked in a few minutes later, he wasn't in any condition for a blow job. And her piercing scream was like a nail through his eye.

Chapter Fourteen

Nash

NASH WOKE UP late and glared bleary-eyed around his motel room. He had liked the cozy feel of home, sleeping in Dolly's bed in her Winnebago. He hadn't liked that she still didn't trust him about what was going on with her. Last year, Nash would have put her on the suspects list because she knew something about the rodeo that she was keeping a secret. He hated to admit it, but her past as an escort might have even colored his opinion a bit.

Except over the past year, he had gotten to know her. She was a good person and she genuinely wanted to succeed in her job. That put her on Shelby's side and so Nash was willing to give her time to come to him. But he was suspicious about what she was hiding. Maybe her future brother-in-law, Shane, wasn't as on the up-and-up as he should have been.

It gutted him that being with Dolly might be a big mistake. Her default was to spin things and work around the rules. His was the exact opposite. He thought he could bend a little about that, but he couldn't. While he realized she might not be ready to tell him that she used to be an escort, she should be able to be honest with him about the investigation they were working on.

He needed her for Laredo, to be his cover while he looked into what the stock suppliers were bringing into the rodeo. She could get him into the back areas and then distract everyone with her smoke and mirror social media show.

Rocky Ridge was coming in from Canada. Jaripeo was coming in from Mexico. And Viking was in the United States. Nash couldn't rule any of them out. And out of all of them, Dolly had a stake in keeping Nash away from Shane and the Viking Ranch.

His phone rang just as he had finished checking out of the motel.

"Hey, Shelby," he said. "I'm heading off to Laredo." He needed to get the lay of the land before the stock suppliers headed into the rodeo grounds this weekend.

"Actually, I need you to come here. To Dallas. To my office. Right now."

Shelby was talking fast and he could hear the panic in her voice.

"What's going on? Did Blevins do something?"

"You need to be here for a meeting at ten."

He cut his eyes to his dashboard clock. He'd barely make it, if he left now and pushed over the speed limit the whole way there. "I'm two hours away and Dallas is in the opposite direction of where I'm going. Are you sure we can't do this over the phone?" he said.

"Positive. It's an emergency."

Shelby didn't use words like emergency unless it really

was one. "Are you all right?"

"I will be once you get here."

"Is it Mom?"

"No."

"Can you talk freely?"

She forced a half-laugh. "No."

"Are you in danger?"

"No," she said more seriously.

"Is it Dad?"

Shelby hesitated. "It's complicated."

Fuck. Of course it was. "I'll be there as soon as I can."

As soon as it was safe, he turned around and put his foot down on the gas. He wasn't sure what time Dolly got into the office, but she didn't answer her phone when he called. It was early but it had gone right to voicemail.

He tried to ignore the sick feeling in his gut that there was something really wrong in the Dallas headquarters. For shits and giggles, he called Jackson Blevin's office line.

"UPRC," a woman's nasally voice said.

"Who's this?" he asked gruffly, deepening his voice.

"This is Debbi. Who is this?"

"Get me Jackson Blevins."

"Um. He's not available right now."

"Where is he?"

"Do you have an appointment? Because all of his appointments have been canceled today."

Is that right? "Why?" he barked, hoping to intimidate her into answering.

"Who is this?"

"Shane Calland," Nash barked, using Dolly's brother-in-law's name. "From the Viking Ranch. I need to talk to him about Laredo."

"I'll pass along the message to him." And then she hung up on him.

Interesting. Nash considered calling back and saying he was from the other two stock suppliers, but he didn't think he could pull off two different voices.

His phone rang again and this time, he didn't recognize the number. He wondered if it was his father. He pulled the truck over, even though he couldn't really afford to and still make it in time for Shelby's meeting.

"Nash?" It was Finn.

"Why are you up so early?" he asked, annoyed now that he'd pulled over for this.

"I know you're not on the roster for Laredo, but I wanted to give you a heads-up, just in case you get Dolly to sweet-talk them into getting you back on the lists."

Nash hoped it didn't come to that. His back still ached from riding. "What's the heads-up?"

"I just heard from a guy I know about the bulls coming up next week. They've got a seventy-five percent success rate."

Nash whistled. Out of one hundred rides, only twenty-five bull riders went the eight seconds. "Damn."

"That's not all. Ten of them are from a different stock contractor."

"Wait," Nash said, grabbing a pen so he could take notes on a crumpled napkin that had been on the floor. "I thought the UPRC could only use the three stock contractors now."

"Well, I think Jaripeo is accepting a commission to put other stock contractors' bulls in their shipment."

"Anyone going to tell the bosses about this outsourcing?"

"Not unless you want to be labeled a snitch."

Nash clenched his jaw. Yeah, that was exactly what he didn't want to be labeled as. Not here too. "A snitch?" He had to remind himself that Finn didn't know his past as a whistle-blower, and wouldn't understand how much that word stung.

"The other guys aren't thrilled about the unknowns, but what can you do? I'm calling to just give you the heads-up that you might want to sit this rodeo out. Just in case they're too much to handle. No offense."

"Thanks for letting me know," Nash said. This made this shipment even more interesting. "But I'll be there, one way or another. Count on it."

Finn hesitated before responding, clearly worried. "You sure about that? You're not exactly the best bull rider around here, and these bulls are no joke."

"I know," Nash admitted. "But I'm all in." All in investigating these bulls, that was.

"You're crazy, son. That's what I like about you. Hey, how are things with you and Dolly?"

"None of your business," he said, but Nash made sure his tone was lighthearted.

"All righty then. See you in a few days."

The drive was long, but Nash made good time. When he pulled into the large parking lot of the office building, however, he hadn't been expecting an ambulance to be idling by the front doors. He called Dolly again. To his relief, she answered on the first ring this time.

"What's going on in there? There's an ambulance out front."

"Why are you here?" she said.

"Shelby called me in. Said she needed to talk to me. Do you know why?"

"No, but someone just beat the shit out of Blevins," she whispered. "I walked into his office a few moments ago, and he was on the ground bleeding all over the place."

"Are you all right?" Nash got out of the truck. "I'm coming up."

"I'm fine. Hold off for a few until things die down. You don't want anyone to recognize you from the rodeo."

"Yeah, that's probably a good idea. I'll talk to you later." He hung up and called Shelby. If Blevins had just gotten his bell rung, that couldn't have been the reason why Shelby had wanted to have a meeting with him. "Hey, I'm going to need a copy of your security footage from this morning," he said when she answered.

"Where are you?" Shelby's voice was high and nervous.

"Right outside."

"Come in through side door B and meet me in my office."

Dolly had a good point about the danger of him being recognized now that everyone in the building would be on high alert for a new face coming into the building. He was dressed business casual, so it was possible that if there was anyone around from the rodeo, they might not recognize him on a first glance. It wouldn't hold up if one of the bull riders or anyone he worked closely with saw him. No one should be near the headquarters on a Tuesday afternoon. The professional cowboys were either still sleeping in, back at home, or on their way to Laredo to get settled in to work their remote jobs while waiting for the weekend.

He supposed if worse came to worst, Dolly would find a way to put a spin on things.

"You sure about this?" Nash asked.

"Yes," she said and there was something in her voice that made him sprint to the side door.

He was buzzed in almost before his hand reached the handle.

He took the elevator up to Shelby's penthouse office and was relieved that he didn't run into anyone he knew along the way. His hand paused mid-knock on the mahogany door to Shelby's office, the brass nameplate catching the afternoon light. The door swung open before his knuckles could land.

Nash swept his gaze around Shelby's office, taking in the rustic touches—a cowhide rug, a framed sketch of wild mustangs, the rough-hewn beams spanning the ceiling. It suited his sister, grounded yet elegant. Shelby sat behind an antique wooden desk, her brown hair twisted into an elegant chignon. But it was the man sitting across from her that made Nash stop cold.

Miles Garrett swiveled in his chair to face Nash, a smug smile stretching across his angular face. He stood and brushed a hand down his designer suit—Armani, if Nash had to guess. Same overpriced Italian leather shoes. Same Rolex peeking out from under a crisp white cuff.

The arrogant prick looked every inch the career FBI agent. And he had the balls to reach out his hand for Nash to shake.

Trying not to grind his teeth, Nash forced himself to shake his ex-partner's hand.

"Nash. It's been a while."

"This is a surprise," Nash said.

"More than you realize. You know Hector, right?"

Nash realized that there was someone else in the room. He had been so focused on Garrett, he hadn't seen Hector Ortiz seated next to him.

"What the hell is going on here?" Nash asked.

Garrett closed the door and then perched a hip on Shelby's desk. "Have a seat," he said, gesturing to the chair he'd just vacated.

"I'll stand," Nash said. He exchanged a glance with Shelby. She looked confused and scared. Nash's hands clenched into fists. If Garrett was threatening her...

"Hector isn't who you think he is. He's actually an undercover DEA agent nearing the end of a three-year-long operation," Garrett continued, his tone dripping with patronizing patience. "Normally, as you know, we wouldn't be offering up this information, but I'm afraid you're going to screw things up for us. We're trying to bust the Jaripeo Ranch for smuggling, and the new shipment of fighting bulls coming in from Mexico to Laredo's rodeo next week could be the big break we're looking for."

Nash's pulse quickened. He didn't like the idea of working with Garrett again, but if it could bring closure to Shelby, he'd do it. "What about Jackson Blevins? Do you have him on your radar for being involved in the smuggling?"

A condescending smirk played at the corners of Garrett's mouth. "We don't have anything that points to either of the CEOs, your sister or Blevins, as being part of smuggling illegal goods in from Mexico."

Nash was already shaking his head. "Blevins just got carried out of here on a stretcher after being worked over. Where I'm sitting, it looks like he is up to his eyeballs in something dirty."

Garrett waved a dismissive hand. "Maybe yes, maybe no. We'll look into it, sure. But our priority is shutting down the cartel's connections. If we stop one avenue, we save lives."

"You can save the rhetoric. I've heard it. My investigation, though, revolves around uncovering if Jackson Blevins is involved in anything illegal. Have either of you got anything on that?"

Hector and Garrett exchanged a look. "Nothing concrete."

"Can you point me in a direction?"

"No," Garrett said shortly.

Meaning yes, but he wasn't going to tell Nash anything.

"Do you have anything for us you'd like to share?" Garrett asked.

"No," Nash said with the same tone and expression.

Garrett's face darkened. "If you have anything you're keeping from us or if you get in the way of what's going down in Laredo, I'll have you arrested for obstruction."

Nash thought about telling him about Jaripeo subcontracting other stock contractors for the bulls. He was used to being a "snitch" after all. And yet because of the way Garrett was acting, Nash didn't say a word.

Garrett straightened his tie, the fabric slipping through his fingers with practiced ease, his gaze steady on Nash. Hector, standing just a step behind, shifted his weight from one foot to another, a subtle dance of impatience on the worn carpet.

The seconds stretched, bending the moment into something brittle. Finally, Garrett turned toward Hector and nodded toward the door. "We should get going. Lots of preparations to make before Laredo." They left, shutting the door behind them.

Shelby let out a shaky sigh. "He said he used to be your partner."

"Yeah," Nash said.

"He's the one you blew the whistle on, isn't he?"

"He told you that?"

"No, your face just did and the way you two acted together."

Figures. "I won't let him get in the way of our investigation. I'm going to find out what Blevins is involved in and get him kicked out of this company, if not arrested."

Shelby bit her lip, worry etched in the lines of her face. "I know you will, but be careful. I can't afford to bail you out if you get arrested. My credit cards are maxed out as it is."

It eased the knot in his chest that she could still joke around with him. "I'm going to go and search Blevins's office."

"Good luck. They've already been through it."

"They might have missed something." Nash doubted it, but he wanted eyes on the office anyway.

"The coast should be clear. I sent his secretary on a bunch of busy-work errands." Shelby rubbed at her temples.

"Why did you lead me to believe that this had something to do with Dad?" he asked from the doorway.

"When Miles first contacted me and said he was with the FBI, I had assumed it was about Dad. I had no idea it was really about the Jaripeo Ranch."

"So he didn't mention our father at all?"

She shook her head. "No." Opening her desk drawer, she pulled out a bottle of Gentleman Jack whiskey.

"It's ten thirty in the morning," Nash said, sounding to himself like an outraged maiden aunt.

"It's five o'clock somewhere."

Chapter Fifteen

Dolly

DOLLY SAT AT her desk, feeling shell-shocked. She stared at her computer without really seeing it. She hadn't been looking forward to her morning chat with Blevins, but never, in her wildest dreams, had she thought she'd find him face down in a pool of blood. Things got weird after that. She remembered screaming, and people flying out of their offices.

Looking down, she saw that she still hadn't drunk the cup of coffee someone had put in her hand. Taking a sip, she grimaced. It was cold and bitter.

She wondered if Nash was in the building yet. Enough time had passed that he could probably come in. After all, it wasn't as if Blevins was coming back soon. She needed to see him. But he was probably in his meeting with Shelby and she didn't want to disturb him.

Well, she couldn't just sit here. She decided to go back to Blevins's office and check things out for herself. If anyone asked her what she was doing up there, she'd just tell them that she dropped something this morning.

There had to be something—anything—that would

prove that Blevins was up to no good. After all, he said he had been attacked by thieves this morning. She snorted. Yeah, right. Thieves who knew just where his office was and just when to find him. They could have simply jumped him in the parking lot. His ravaged office might hold some clue as to why he was targeted, what they were really after.

She pushed herself away from her desk and headed toward Jackson Blevins's office.

The hallway felt eerily quiet compared to the earlier commotion. As she rounded the corner, she was surprised to see Nash about to let himself into Blevins's office.

Nash looked up when he heard her bearing down on him. He looked up, a faint smile playing at the corners of his lips. "Why am I not surprised?"

Dolly swallowed hard against the knot of awareness blooming in her throat as their gazes met and held. "I'm here to help."

"You shouldn't be here," he said.

"Why should you have all the fun? Besides, it'll go faster with both of us looking."

"True," he conceded with bad grace. His gaze flickered to her mouth for the briefest second before he looked away.

"What could go wrong?"

Nash's eyes narrowed at her flippant remark. "You saw what happened to Blevins. This isn't some game."

Dolly lifted her chin, refusing to let him see her nerves. "Standing around guessing won't get us any answers either. And the longer we stay out here bickering about it, the more chance someone's going to come along and ask what we're doing."

He studied her for a long moment before giving a curt nod of acceptance. "Fine. But you stick close and do exactly as I say, understood?"

The commanding edge to his tone sent a shiver through her, though Dolly couldn't be certain whether it was from trepidation or something else entirely. She nodded.

Holding her gaze for a beat longer, Nash finally broke away to slide a key card into the door. The panel lights wobbled between red and green before reading a steady green light. At the audible click, Nash opened the door and slipped inside, Dolly on his heels.

"That's a handy little device," she said.

"When I first started, Shelby scored me a master key card. I've been through his office a few times. I haven't found anything on his computer, and he doesn't keep any paper files. But maybe this time around, he was careless."

"That sounds like wishful thinking to me."

"Me too, but I'm trying to remain positive. I haven't had a lot of wins in the past year, either inside or outside of the ring."

"You'll get there. You're too stubborn to let Blevins get away with hurting Shelby and the rodeo."

The office was a study in opulence, all gleaming mahogany and leather. Thick Persian rugs muffled their footsteps as they crept inside, closing the door behind them. The room smelled of expensive leather and ambition, an unmistakable aura of power emanating from the dark wood-paneled walls.

Papers were still strewn about. Blevins's phone sat

slightly askew where it had been knocked off the hook.

"Whoever did this wasn't messing around," Nash muttered under his breath.

"Do you really think it was corporate thieves after something?"

Nash snorted. "No."

Dolly looked around nervously. "Do you think they'll be back?"

"Depends on who they are. If they work here, they could have just gone back to their desks."

"That's chilling." She tried not to shiver. "Why do you think they beat him up?"

"He pissed off the wrong person." Nash scanned the room. His gaze lingered on the massive oak desk situated in front of floor-to-ceiling windows that overlooked the city skyline. "He liked to show off, whether it was by throwing money around or having this cushy office."

Dolly's lips twisted. "Compensating for something, no doubt."

Nash huffed out a quiet laugh, the sound sending a spark down Dolly's spine. "Let's see if we can find out why Blevins got tuned up this morning."

Nash made a beeline for the desk, while Dolly quietly investigated the shelves and cabinets lining the walls. As Nash rifled through the scattered papers, his brows furrowed in concentration. "Anything interesting over there?"

Dolly shook her head, her fingers tracing the spines of some books that were still on the shelf. "Nothing yet. Everything seems pretty standard."

As Nash logged into Blevins's computer, typing a code

Shelby must have given him, Dolly sat on the floor and dumped out the trash bin. Sifting through discarded papers, she searched for anything that might connect Blevins to anything hinky.

"There's some new emails that came through that might give us some more information. He hasn't had a chance to read them or scrub them from the computer yet." Nash plugged an external drive into the computer. "I'm copying all his files onto this, so I can go through them later."

"Good idea," Dolly replied, her eyes narrowing as she spotted something at the bottom of the trash bin—a crumpled invoice with a familiar logo. Her pulse quickened as she unfolded the paper. It was a bill from Jaripeo Ranch, addressed to Jackson personally, with a list of items that appeared to be coded because she didn't recognize any of the words.

"Nash, look at this," she whispered, holding up the invoice for him to see. "It's from Jaripeo. It may be about the bulls. But it's not in Spanish or English."

"I'll take that," he said, snatching it out of her hand and pocketing it in his pants.

"Maybe Hector Ortiz knows what this is all about."

"Leave Hector alone. I'll take care of it."

"Do you think this is proof that Jaripeo is smuggling?"

"I think you need to stay out of this. If Blevins is smuggling things in from Mexico, I guarantee you it's not tequila."

Dolly was going to argue with him, but the sound of footsteps approaching down the hall made them both freeze. Her heart hammered in her chest as she recognized the voice of Debbi, Blevin's secretary, chatting animatedly on the phone.

"Quick, in the closet," Nash whispered.

Dolly shoved all the garbage back into the can and scurried to her feet. Nash pulled her into a small closet beside the bookshelves. They ducked inside and closed the door, just as Debbi entered the office, still absorbed in her conversation.

"Give me a sec," Debbi said into the phone, oblivious that they were hiding mere feet away. "What a freakin' mess it is in here. And I bet you can guess who has to clean it."

Dolly and Nash exchanged a frustrated look as they squeezed themselves together in between a suit jacket and a beaded evening gown. What the actual hell was that for?

"I've got to check Jackson's calendar. He forgot to sync the damned thing."

Dolly peeked through the slats in the door and saw Debbi plunk herself into his desk chair.

"The drive," Dolly whispered, barely breathing the word into Nash's ear.

He moved his mouth, his lips brushing against her cheekbone, and he breathed back. "I've got it."

Dolly sagged against him. Cramped in here together, it was hard to stand. She clung to him for support. Their close proximity sent a jolt of awareness through her, but she pushed it aside, focusing on the task at hand.

"Got it," Debbi said. "He wanted me to delete all this junk mail that came in today. I don't know why that's so damned important that he had to call me from the hospital to do it right now." She leaned back and put her feet on the desk. "Yeah, I've got a few minutes. Spill the tea. No one is telling me anything."

Dolly closed her eyes and resisted the urge to groan. This was going to take a while.

"The story I got was some thugs followed him in from the parking lot and robbed him." There was a pause and then Debbi said, "I don't know, but the FBI confiscated the security tapes so they'll catch them."

"FBI?" Dolly whispered.

Nash rolled his eyes and mouthed the word "later."

The sound of their breathing filled the small space, mingling with the scent of his aftershave. Dolly could feel the heat emanating from Nash's body, a steady warmth that both comforted and excited her.

Debbi's side of the conversation carried snippets of gossip and office politics, but nothing that provided any insight into Jackson's illicit activities.

OMG why won't she shut up?

"One sec, I've got another call coming through," Debbi said. "Yes, Mr. Blevins, I just received a call from our contact at the bank. They said the funds haven't cleared yet, but should be available by tomorrow morning."

Funds? What funds?

She and Nash exchanged a significant look. This could be the big break they were looking for. They should have hid in a closet a long time ago.

"Yes, sir, I understand. The money will be transferred to the offshore account as soon as it clears. No one will suspect a thing. I'll delete everything as usual." A few clicks of the keyboard later, Debbi said, "Okay, I'm back."

After an eternity, Debbi wrapped up her conversation and left the office, closing the door behind her. They eased out of the closet and Dolly went to the door while Nash went to the desk.

"I think I can save the data she just tried to purge."

Dolly's legs were shaking with adrenaline as she glanced down the hallway. "The coast is clear."

"Let's stop pushing our luck and get out of here."

As they hurried down the corridor out of the executive suite, Nash's hand was warm against her back. "This is good right?"

"It's good," he said. "But don't get your hopes up just yet."

"What did Debbi mean that the FBI has the security tapes? They were here?"

"Yeah, that was the meeting Shelby wanted me in here for today." Nash sighed hard out of his nose. "I can't say much, but they're very much interested in things right now."

"Can they help us nail Blevins?"

Nash shrugged and didn't answer.

"What type of things are they looking at?" she asked, dying of curiosity.

"I can't say."

She had a feeling that he wouldn't say, but then again they were in the middle of the office where anyone could hear them. "What does that mean for our investigation?"

"My investigation," he said.

Ouch. But she supposed she deserved that for keeping secrets from him. "Well?" she demanded.

"Nothing changes for Laredo. I'm your VIP. You get me back-area access and I'll take it from there."

"There's something you're not telling me," she said.

"How does it feel?"

She winced. "Yeah, not too good."

He reached down to hold her hand. "You need to trust me so I can trust you."

She nodded. "I'm getting up the nerve."

"You?" Nash scoffed. "You're fearless."

"Only when the camera is on," she said.

He turned her to face him, his hands comforting on her upper arms. "You're a force to be reckoned with and you're going to help turn this rodeo into one of the greatest in the country."

She smiled at that image. "That's a high expectation."

"Not for you. It's a piece of cake for someone with your skills."

"If you say so." Dolly could almost believe him when she looked into his sincere and caring eyes. She needed to tell him about her escort days so she could move on and concentrate on the stuff that really mattered. But the thought made her stomach churn like a mechanical bull gone haywire. Her throat tightened at the thought of seeing judgment and disgust in his eyes. Stepping into his arms, she laid her head on his chest. It felt so good to be hugged, so good not to have to be the one in control or in charge for a moment. Would Nash protect her and stand by her if she got fired from UPRC if her escort days came up? What if their romance was over before it even got a chance to start? She desperately wanted to believe he would.

"I've got to get out of here and work on the information on the drive," he said. "Keep your head down. Better yet, why don't you take an early day and work from your apartment or the Winnebago."

"No," she said, shaking her head. "I can't. I've got a sponsor coming in this afternoon."

"Okay. Be safe. I'll be hanging around Dallas until Shelby gets sick of me. Can I see you tonight?"

"Yeah, I'd like that." She'd really like that. She'd tell him about the cheerleading uniform she received. If she couldn't tell him about Leisure Industries, she could just tell him that the gift made her feel uncomfortable and sexualized. That was mostly the truth. It would be a start.

"Me too," he said, although he looked a little wistful when he said it. He dropped a quick kiss on her mouth and took a sharp left to get to the elevator.

She wanted to call him back and have him stick around a little longer. Things didn't seem so bad when he was around, and she didn't feel as alone and vulnerable. She didn't think the people who assaulted Blevins would be back, and even if they did, there wasn't any reason why they would seek her out. But it didn't feel safe being in the office today.

Forcing herself to snap out of it, Dolly's gaze shifted to the computer screen and its long list of emails, each demanding her full attention. That should be enough of a distraction. Right now, she needed to be the social maven that she had been hired to be. She had a sponsor meeting to prepare for.

As she tried to work, her phone buzzed insistently. She flicked her eyes to the wall of texts that were being sent. Jackson Blevins must be bored in his hospital bed. When she ignored the texts, her phone started to ring. She let it go to voicemail, but the phone rang again, skittering across the laminate surface of her desk.

"Mr. Blevins, I don't have time for this right now. I have a potential sponsor coming in any minute."

His voice oozed through the speaker, as smooth and noxious as an oil slick. "When you're finished with them, you need to come to my hospital room."

"Why?" Dolly asked, leaning back in her chair. "I'm sure Debbi can help you with whatever you need."

"Debbi's not you. I need your...special touch in a private matter."

Oh ugh. Dolly made a face. Bile rose in her throat at the innuendo lacing his words. She hoped she was imagining things, but she knew she wasn't. She wished she could record this conversation for the record. Instead, she just scribbled down notes for the report she and Shelby were working on to present to the board about his inappropriate behaviors.

"I'm not your secretary. If you need something, ask Debbi. I've got work to do." Without waiting for his response, Dolly ended the call and blocked his number for good. She'd dance with the devil when she had to, but she sure as hell wasn't going to let him lead. Besides, if everything went according to plan, Jackson Blevins might not be CEO for much longer—and she couldn't wait for that day.

She couldn't afford any more distractions. Not when she needed to nail this sponsorship deal. There was business to attend to and she wasn't going to let personal matters derail her professional game.

Pocketing her phone, Dolly stood up and went to get a cup of coffee for a distraction from Blevins's nonsense. On the way to the breakroom, she passed by Debbi who was hurrying back to her desk while "Yes sirring" someone, probably Blevins.

As she waited for her coffee to brew, Dolly rested a hip against the counter and allowed her mind to wander to more pleasant things. Like Nash's touch that still lingered on her skin, a phantom sensation that sent shivers down her spine. She thought about his calloused hands skimming over her skin, igniting sparks in their wake. She couldn't wait to feel the rasp of his stubble against her inner thigh. A delicious ache bloomed deep in her core.

And then her phone buzzed again and jolted her out of the nice little fantasy she was building.

"What?" she snapped into the phone.

"Lonestar Leathercraft is here to see you," the receptionist said.

"Send them up," Dolly said. And then wondered if the men who beat up Blevins had snuck into the building or if Jackson had authorized them to come up. Guess she'd have to wait until she spoke to Nash and see if he had seen the surveillance tapes or if he could use his former ties at the FBI to get a copy of them.

Dolly headed to the elevator bank so she could greet Martha Simmons from Lonestar Leathercraft right away.

They had spoken on the phone and sent texts back and forth, but this would be the first time they met in person.

The elevator doors opened and a well-dressed woman in her mid-fifties held out her hand. "Ms. Keller? I'm Martha. Thank you for taking the time to meet with us."

Us?

Any words she had died in her throat as a familiar figure stepped out from behind Martha. Tall and lean, with salt-and-pepper hair and knowing brown eyes, Jefferson Laker looked every inch the successful businessman.

And the last person Dolly expected to see in her office.

Dolly numbly shook Martha's offered hand.

"I wanted to introduce you to our partial owner, Jefferson Laker."

"Hello," Dolly managed.

"Ms. Keller," Jefferson said with a small nod.

Her mind raced through scenarios, each one ending with her secret laid bare before the unforgiving UPRC rodeo community.

She forced a smile. "Can I get you two any coffee?"

"No, we're on a tight schedule," Jefferson said.

Martha nodded apologetically.

"Well, let's get down to business then," Dolly said, and gestured them toward her office. Was this just a coincidence? Or had Jefferson known that she was working on this deal? He had been a decent man all those years ago; she shouldn't be jumping to conclusions about his intentions. And yet, her experiences with Jackson Blevins had colored her expectations about rich men's behaviors.

Chapter Sixteen

Dolly

A FTER DOLLY WRAPPED up her presentation, Jefferson looked over at Martha and said, "Would you mind if I spoke to Ms. Keller privately?"

Dolly's heart stuttered in her chest.

"Of course," Martha said. "I think I'll take you up on that offer of coffee now."

"It's right around the corner," Dolly said through numb lips.

When Martha left, the click of the door latch sounded like a gunshot in the stillness of the office.

Dolly sat down at the conference room table.

"I was surprised to hear your name from Finn," Jefferson said, thumbing through a stack of brochures that showcased the upcoming events. "You've done well for yourself."

"I've worked hard to get where I am." She lifted her chin, meeting his stare head-on. "And I'm not going to let anything jeopardize that."

"Easy." He held up his hands in a placating gesture. "I'm not here to cause trouble. I just wanted to see you again. See how things worked out for you. Finn loved the photo shoot that you did with him. It was very professional."

Despite the tension coiled in her gut, Dolly felt a flicker of pride. "Thank you. Finn makes it easy. He's really making a name for himself on the rodeo circuit, isn't he?"

"Sure is." Jefferson beamed with pride. "He's got more talent than I ever did. I reckon he'll be one of the greats someday."

"I don't doubt that for a second."

He hesitated for a moment before continuing the conversation. "Listen, I know we have a complicated history, but I'd like to put that behind us. I'm happy to see that you're doing well. I've thought about you often over the years. You're a strong woman, and you deserve every success that comes your way."

Dolly had to fight to blink back tears. That was unexpected. "Thank you," she said quietly.

"Anyhow…" Jefferson glanced at his watch, a flicker of regret crossing his face "…I hate to cut this short, but I've got another meeting to attend to."

"Of course." Dolly got up and smoothed down her skirt.

They walked through the busy office. Martha joined them as they passed by the break room.

"Martha, Lonestar Leathercraft will be sponsoring ten athletes of Dolly's choice. We'll work out the details later."

Dolly did blink back tears this time. "That's incredibly generous. Thank you. UPRC has no shortage of gifted athletes. I can put together a list of popular riders who'll be more than happy to have a Lonestar Leathercraft saddle."

"Excellent," Martha said.

With a final nod at Dolly, Jefferson walked into the elevator with Martha.

Dolly let out a big sigh. She had kept her secret safe and secured a major sponsorship deal. Not bad for a day's work. It was a bit of a relief that Jefferson Laker was still the nice guy that she remembered.

Now all she had to do was get through the rest of the day and then she could enjoy her night with Nash. But as she made her way back to her desk, Dolly's eyes flicked to Debbi's empty desk. With a glance around, she confirmed that no one was looking directly at her. She eased into Debbi's office and quietly closed the door behind her.

When she jiggled the mouse, the screen appeared. Luckily, it didn't ask for a password. The first thing Dolly wanted to do was get her hands on the staffing information for the Laredo rodeo. The preliminary email had circulated this morning, which is how she knew Nash's name hadn't been on the VIP list, but the final version wouldn't be sent out until later. It was a piece of cake to open up the document and add Nash's name so his VIP badge would be available at the will-call booth this time. She sent the email with the word "Final" in the subject line. If Blevins could send out promo packages from her email, turnabout was fair play and she could send out information from his office as well.

With Nash's name safely on the Laredo list, Dolly was about to cover her tracks and go back to her own office. But the thought of that offshore account that Debbi had mentioned gnawed at her. She decided she could afford to snoop around a bit more. She navigated through a labyrinth of digital files, searching for any hint of illicit financial activity. File after file opened and closed, revealing nothing but mundane transactions and tedious bookkeeping. It was boring and frustrating, and she was risking getting caught the longer she sat here.

A prompt flashed up. Debbi just got a new email from Blevins by the looks of it. But she couldn't access it without a password. She tried a few generic guesses, all meeting with rejection. With a huff, Dolly stopped attempting to hack her way into Debbi's email. She didn't want to lock Debbi out of the system.

She was covering her tracks and erasing the history when she caught sight of a file she had missed before. It was marked DK6969. It struck her as being the type of thing that Blevins would name a file. She opened it, skimming through the contents.

"Fuck," she whispered, feeling the world tilt.

DK was her. Dolly Keller.

There in cold, unforgiving black and white were the details of her employment history at Leisure Industries. Scanned pictures of the catalog that Leisure had sent out with her featured in it were in the file. Shame burst through her, like hot vomit. Her family would be mortified if they saw these cheesecake pictures. And Nash? He'd be disgusted. She was disgusted.

She stared at the screen, the words blurring together. She saw a receipt for the cheerleader uniform. Blevins knew. He had been the one to send it. That made total sense. The "How much?" card was something he would do. Why hadn't she figured that out before now? She was supposed to be smart.

Just what was he planning to do with this information? Was the whole reason he sent the cheerleading outfit and the "How much?" card because he was serious about hiring her as an escort? Or did he plan to somehow blackmail her with the information?

Who else aside from Debbi and Blevins had seen this? Did Shelby know?

Panic clawed at her insides, threatening to consume her. She deleted the file. And then emptied the trash. It was gone from the computer, but not from existence, not from the minds of whoever had already read it.

She had to get out of here. Hurrying out of Debbi's office, she kept her head down as she went back to her own. After gathering up her things, she ran out of the building. She wanted nothing more than to go home and throw herself down on her bed and scream into her pillow.

Unfortunately, when she got home Loretta was painting in her apartment. She looked up when Dolly burst through the door.

"I thought you'd be in the Winnebago," Dolly said, realizing that she hadn't bothered to hide the emotion on her face.

Loretta put her paintbrush down. "The light's better here. What's the matter?"

Dolly forced a bright smile. "Nothing."

"Cut the crap."

And because Dolly didn't have anything close to her

usual defenses left to fall back on, she did. She told Loretta everything, from the moment she got canned from the cheerleading squad all the way up to seeing Jefferson Laker and finding the catalog on Jackson Blevins's computer.

Loretta handed her a glass of sweet tea and a tuna salad sandwich with a plate of chips. Dolly blinked at it.

"I'm not hungry," she said.

"Have you eaten anything today?"

No. Dolly grudgingly ate a potato chip and then scarfed the sandwich down while Loretta watched.

"Do you hate me?" Dolly asked when she finished.

"Don't be an ass. Did you hate me when I screwed up my marriage?"

"No, but that wasn't your fault and neither was your affair with your art professor." Dolly leaned back on the couch. "I, on the other hand, knew what I was doing."

"You fucked up. Guess what? You're human."

Dolly gave her a painful smile. "Are you going to tell Mom and Dad?"

"It's not on my list of conversations to have with them, no." Loretta sat across from her and put her stockinged feet up on the coffee table. Dolly resisted the urge to bat them down—after all her older sister did make her lunch.

"But you need to tell Nash, just so he hears it from you."

"I know. I'm planning on it tonight. Do you think he'll think differently about me?"

"If he does, he's not worth your heart. Because it's leading that way, isn't it?"

Dolly gave a slow nod. "I really like him. He's funny."

"He's a grump."

"He's honest and a decent man."

"That's not a high bar," Loretta said. "I should know. Look at the losers I've been with."

"What about Taylor?"

"Taylor's different." She gave a self-conscious smile. "I really like him too."

Dolly wondered if Taylor had given her the turquoise necklace yet, which he got from Hector Ortiz. "I really like the fact that I can always trust Nash to do the right thing. He is loyal and kind, but I think he might have too rigid an outlook on life for me."

"You haven't really given him a chance," Loretta pointed out.

"There hasn't been a lot of time. I've been so focused on making the UPRC successful so I'll have a permanent place in the business that there hasn't been a lot of time for anything else."

"All jobs are temporary. It doesn't matter how good you are, sometimes shit happens."

"Yeah, I'm just worried that if shit happens, I'll be back at Leisure Industries."

"No, you won't. I won't allow it. We've got the Winnebago so you'll never be homeless and your type of job allows you to work anywhere in the world. If worse comes to worst, you can try and build your brand again. This time not with makeup tutorials or any of that shit. You can do a travel blog about life in an RV. That's really popular right now." Loretta flashed her phone at her and scrolled through the reels. "I'm not saying it's an ideal solution, but it's one you can do without letting billionaires grope you."

Dolly chuckled. "They didn't grope me."

"That's because you probably intimidated the hell out of them."

"Hey," she said and kicked out at Loretta's feet. Loretta quickly moved them to the floor.

"And I know that Mom and Dad would let you move in with them until you get back on your feet again. Ask me how I know?" she said sadly.

Loretta had been living with them ever since her divorce.

"I'm worried though if it comes out that I was an escort, LeAnn could lose her sponsorship."

"If she does, you'll find her another one."

"You have a lot of confidence in me," Dolly said.

"That's because I've seen you in action."

Dolly nodded. "You know, I feel a little bit better. It's a huge relief not to have to carry this all alone. I'm going to tell Nash tonight and I think it's going to be okay. Hopefully, I deleted the only copy of that awful file and by the time Jackson Blevins is out of the hospital, he'll have other issues to think about."

"What about his secretary?"

"Debbi hasn't said anything so far. She might not have seen it. She might not even care." Dolly thought that was probably wishful thinking, but she didn't want to dwell on it.

"You should have told me sooner," Loretta said.

"I couldn't. I was too ashamed and I didn't want to disappoint anyone."

"I'm your sister. I'll love you no matter what. Don't you feel the same?"

"Of course I do." Dolly got up and gave her sister a hug. "But your ass has to be out of here by dinner tonight. Nash and I have a date and hopefully he'll still be here for breakfast."

Chapter Seventeen

Nash

THE RIGHT THING to do was contact Miles about the data from the external drive he had taken from Blevins's office and get the bureau's help in figuring out the coded invoice from the Jaripeo Ranch. He was pretty sure that had something to do with the subcontractors who were supplying the Mexican fighting bulls. And possibly the smuggling operation that Hector and Miles were working on. The FBI could also aid in tracking down that offshore account that Debbi had referred to in her phone call with Blevins. So why was he hesitating picking up the phone?

Because Miles was the reason he was no longer an agent and he wanted petty revenge or to feel superior. So he allowed himself a good fifteen minutes of self-righteousness before he got over himself and called the number on the business card Miles gave to Shelby.

"I hadn't expected to hear from you so soon," Miles said by way of greeting.

"I'm not backing down from my investigation of Jackson Blevins," Nash said. "But I've got copies of his computer data that you might find interesting in your case.

I also overheard a conversation between Miles and his secretary, Debbi Mitchell." Nash checked the notes he had written up. "She said to him something along the lines of the money will be transferred to the offshore account as soon as it clears. No one will suspect a thing. She'll delete everything as usual."

"Interesting," Garrett said. "Anything else?"

Snitch.

"Yeah, we found a coded bill to Blevins from the Jaripeo Ranch. I was informed by one of the bull riders that Jaripeo is subcontracting to other breeders to bring in Mexican fighting bulls for the Laredo rodeo."

"And you are, of course, going to give that invoice to us." It wasn't a question.

"I would like the courtesy of seeing the security tapes from today."

"How about I just give you the pictures of the two men who worked over Blevins?"

"And any information that you have on them."

"I don't have to share any of this with you. You're not local law enforcement."

"No, but I am a licensed private investigator who has been hired by the UPRC to find out if Blevins is involved in anything illegal. I have a duty to my client to protect her interests."

"Your sister, you mean."

"My client."

"Like I was helping my family and friends," he said.

Oh here we go.

"The key difference, Miles, is I'm on a case. You were

just violating human rights and breaking the law."

For a moment Nash thought he had gone too far, but then Garrett burst into a sharp laugh. "You haven't changed. I'm not the bad guy here."

"Prove it."

"We can exchange the information tonight."

"I have plans tonight."

"Take it or leave it, Weaver."

Shit. Dolly would understand why he had to delay their date until after his meeting with Miles. "When and where?" he asked resigned to the fact that he'd have to spend time with his old partner.

"I'll be here at five p.m." Miles rattled off an address in Austin, about three hours away.

"Really?" Best-case scenario he'd be back in Dallas by nine or ten. He hoped Dolly would still be up.

"We need to be on our way to Laredo. This is on the way."

"Fine."

"Look, I get why you did what you did. I was in the wrong, but it was for the right reason. Sometimes you need to bend the rules, especially when the bad guys don't care about them at all."

He sounded like Dolly when he talked like that.

"The rules exist for a reason."

Yeah, that even sounded priggish to him. He must have changed a bit in the last year on the rodeo tour.

"I just want you to know that I don't have any hard feelings. I had nothing to do with how the office treated you. I transferred out, remember."

"Yeah, I remember."

"You were a good agent and I'm sorry you didn't feel that you could stay."

"Thanks," Nash said grudgingly.

"And who knows, maybe the bureau could use a free-lancer with your skills. Where's your brick-and-mortar office?"

Good question. "We can talk about that tonight." Nash hung up on him. He wasn't sure how he felt about all of that. He didn't want to owe Garrett anything, and he certainly didn't want to beg for scraps from him. Nope. He wasn't going to get his hopes up. He wasn't going to be indebted to Miles. And he wasn't ready to forgive him either. But it raised a good question. Where was he going to end up when all this was over?

If Shelby still had a rodeo when it all shook down, Nash supposed he could settle down here in Dallas where she had her headquarters. It had always been her and him against the world anyways. He liked the idea of staying close to her and making sure she was safe from men like Blevins.

Bonus points that Dolly had an apartment in Dallas too, when she wasn't on the road following the rodeos for her social media events. Even though they had been dancing around their attraction for the better part of a year, it was crazy to start thinking about the future after one passionate encounter. And yet, his thoughts kept drifting to her and the future they might share together, if she stopped lying to him.

Her phone went to voicemail, so Nash left her a message that he wouldn't be available until after nine p.m. tonight for their date.

NASH GRIPPED THE steering wheel of his Ford pickup, the leather beneath his fingers growing slick with the sweat of frustration. The endless stretch of Texas highway rolled out before him as he drove back to Dallas. He couldn't shake the feeling that he'd been given the short end of the stick. The FBI had confiscated all the evidence he'd painstakingly collected against Jackson Blevins. In return, he'd been handed a grainy security camera photo of two burly men. Nash didn't recognize them, and Miles said that Blevins—conveniently enough—claimed not to know them either.

At least Miles agreed to deploy the FBI's resources to track down the offshore account connected to Jackson Blevins and work on the encrypted code from the invoice from Jaripeo Ranch he and Dolly had fished out of Blevins's trash can. They said they had installed tracking software on Blevins and his secretary Debbi's computers.

Nash doubted they would share anything that they found out with him, though.

Blevins would remain in the hospital for a few more days, which would give the FBI more time to work on the case and set up a sting at the Laredo rodeo. Not that Nash would be a part of that. It pissed him off. If he had still been in the bureau...but he wasn't. He was a private eye, and he should feel lucky Miles was even giving him the time of day. Yeah, that stung like a bitch.

Nash knew he had to get over himself. Still, he couldn't shake the sour taste of regret on his tongue. Walking away from his credentials had cost him access to resources. If someone had told him a few years ago that he'd be playing cowboy and sneaking around behind the FBI's back, he'd have laughed in their face. But here he was forging deals with his old partner to help Shelby untangle this mess with Blevins.

It was worth it. Shelby hadn't deserved a partner like Blevins. With him out of the picture, Nash knew she would make the rodeo thrive.

But if Nash was being fair, the meeting with Miles hadn't been so bad. He had built him up as an evil villain in his life's story, but the reality was Miles was a good agent. He generally wanted to do good, but his methods were what got him into trouble. He was an "ends justifies the means" type of guy and Nash just wasn't wired that way.

It had been uncomfortable sitting in the meeting room with him and Hector as they exchanged information and realizing that Miles and Dolly would probably get along. Dolly was an "ends justifies the means" type as well.

While Nash would never be that casual about breaking the rules, he could see how tempting it would be in a situation like they were in right now. Which was why he had to double down and make sure everyone did this by the book, so there wasn't any way in hell that Jackson Blevins could weasel himself out of anything this time.

Just as he was about to call Dolly and tell him his ETA, Nash's phone buzzed. He glanced at the caller ID on the truck's display. Dr. Victor Lance. That was interesting.

"Dr. Lance," he said, "what can I do for you?"

"Mr. Weaver," Lance replied, his voice trembling slightly, "I heard about Jackson Blevins being put in the hospital, and I think it's finally safe for me to talk."

Nash felt a spark of excitement, realizing he didn't need to build a criminal case against Blevins. All he had to do was provide proof to Shelby that Blevins had been involved with illegal activity, and Lance's information just might be the break he was looking for. He could do this without Miles. And wouldn't that be gratifying as all get-out?

"I'm listening," he said, keeping his tone neutral despite the adrenaline surging through his veins.

"I want immunity."

"I'm not a lawyer. I can't guarantee any specific outcome."

"Okay."

"You should talk to your lawyer."

"I have. She agrees that coming clean about my dealings with Blevins is the best course of action. I want to meet with you tonight, before I lose my nerve."

Tonight?

Shit, he was almost halfway back to Dallas. And to Dolly. Figured. "I can be at your motel in a few hours."

"I'll be here."

He had been looking forward to spending the night with Dolly, but as much as he hated to admit it, the meeting with Lance had to take precedence.

"Call Dolly," he told the voice-activated feature on his phone.

As the phone rang, he rehearsed his words in his head, trying to find the right balance between conveying the urgency of the situation and expressing his regret for the last-minute change of plans.

"Hey there, cowboy." Dolly's voice sounded strained, lacking her usual playful lilt.

Nash frowned, his instincts immediately picking up on her distress. "Is everything okay? You sound a bit off."

She sighed, the sound crackling through the phone's speaker. "It's just been a long day at the office. Nothing to worry about. I'm looking forward to seeing you."

Nash's stomach twisted with guilt. "About that...I have some news."

He briefly explained the situation with Dr. Lance. As he spoke, he could almost feel Dolly's disappointment radiating through the phone. "I know this isn't ideal, but I wouldn't be doing this if it wasn't important. We're so close to exposing Blevins, and I need to follow this lead."

There was a moment of silence on the other end of the line. Nash held his breath, waiting for Dolly's response.

"No, you're right. You've got to do this. I wish I could be there too."

"I'll make it up to you."

"You better," she teased, a hint of her usual spirit returning. "Just be careful, okay? I don't want to lose you just when things are starting to get interesting between us."

Nash smiled, warmth spreading through his chest at her words. "I'll be careful. And when this is all over, we'll have all the time in the world to explore just how interesting things can get."

"Have a nice night."

"You too, sweetheart."

Nash stopped to gas up and pick up some coffee to keep himself going. After what seemed like an eternity driving down the highway, Lance's motel loomed ahead, its flashing neon sign a beacon in the gathering darkness. Nash parked the truck and took a deep breath, steeling himself for the conversation to come.

He knocked on the door, three sharp raps that echoed in the stillness. It cracked open, revealing a haggard face etched with fear and exhaustion. Lance peered out, his bloodshot eyes widening as he recognized Nash. He stepped aside, allowing Nash to enter the dimly lit room.

The door clicked shut behind Nash. Lance glanced at the window one more time before turning his attention back to Nash. The room was tidy, but the signs of a prolonged stay were evident—clothes strewn about, empty takeout containers, and a laptop occupying the small desk in the corner.

"Can I get you something to drink?" Lance asked, gesturing to the mini fridge. "Got some beer in here."

"Thanks, but no."

"I wasn't sure you'd come."

"I'm here. Now, let's talk about what you know."

Lance took a long swig of his beer. "I'm sorry about Mick and Ronnie," he said, his voice trembling. "I drugged their bulls. I did it for money and because Jackson said he would fire me if I didn't."

"How much did he give you?" Nash already knew there weren't any large payments in Lance's bank account.

"I got a thousand dollars cash for each one." Lance's gaze dropped to the floor. "You have to believe me. I didn't think anything would happen to the bull riders. Mick was a professional and Ronnie was just the best. The steroids I injected into the bulls should have just made for a harder ride. They were supposed to get thrown, not maimed and killed."

Nash fought to keep his revulsion from showing on his face. He needed Lance to keep talking. "Where's the money?"

"Spent it," Lance said with a bitter half-laugh. "On nothing, really. It's all gone."

Two thousand dollars. Two men's lives upended—one gone forever—over a sum that couldn't even buy you a decent used car. "Why didn't you come clean and tell everyone what Blevins threatened you with?"

A shudder ran through Lance's body. "He said he'd kill me if I did."

Now they were getting somewhere. "And you believed him?"

Lance's face paled. "I did. I've seen the guys who do his dirty work. Blevins has two thugs that he uses as enforcers."

"Do you know their names?"

Lance shook his head. "Big guys. Nasty pieces of work."

"Could you identify them if you saw them again?"

"Yeah."

Playing a hunch, Nash pulled out the grainy security picture Miles had given him and held it up. "Are these the guys?"

Lance's eyes widened as he stared at the image. "That's

them."

Blevins must have tried a double cross or something, and that was why his own men went after him. But with Lance testifying that these guys were Blevins's enforcers and he had used them to intimidate people and had threatened to kill him if he didn't dope up the bulls, that was all Shelby needed to take to the board. He'd let Miles and the FBI sort through the rest.

It was over. Or else it soon would be.

"I need you to type out exactly what you just told me and email it to me. Every detail, no matter how small."

Lance hesitated for a moment before nodding. He grabbed his laptop and began typing.

Nash watched him. This was it. The breakthrough they'd been waiting for. Blevins was going down. And Nash wouldn't even need the FBI's help to do it.

After Lance hit send, Nash confirmed the email's arrival in his inbox. He handed Lance Garrett's business card. "Contact him if you think of anything else."

Lance took the card with a shaking hand.

Nash stood. "I'm not sure what will happen next, but your cooperation might work in your favor when this goes to court."

With that, Nash left the motel room.

He got in the truck and reached for his phone, his fingers hovering over Dolly's number. He wanted to hear her voice, to share the news of his breakthrough. But he hesitated, glancing at the clock on the dashboard. It was late, and she was probably already asleep. He didn't want to wake her.

As he pulled onto the highway, he rubbed his eyes, willing away the fatigue that threatened to overtake him. It had been a long day, and an even longer investigation, but the end was finally in sight. It was close to one a.m. by the time he pulled back into Dallas. He'd call both Shelby and Dolly tomorrow and share the good news. Right now, he just wanted to grab a cheap motel room and sleep for hours.

Chapter Eighteen

Dolly

THE NEXT MORNING, Dolly thought about calling into work and just lounging in bed all day. But she had decided last night, after eating a pint of Ben & Jerry's, that she was going to tell Shelby about her escort past. Loretta had a good point. There were people who needed to hear the news from her first.

Of course, she'd ask Shelby not to say anything to Nash until she had a chance to talk to him. She hoped that she still had a job after telling Shelby that if news spread about her working at Leisure Industries, she'd be in violation of her morality clause in her contract.

Taking a steadying breath, Dolly checked her makeup in the mirror and attempted to smooth her tousled hair into some semblance of order. A harsh knock on her door surprised her. It was barely eight a.m. Could it be Nash coming by for a good-morning kiss?

But when she pulled open the door, it wasn't Nash standing there, but a stern-faced stranger in a crisp suit flashing a badge.

"Special Agent Miles Garrett, FBI. We need to talk,

Ms. Keller."

"Um, come in, I guess. I was just heading to the office."

Miles didn't so much as blink at her obvious confusion. He also stayed in the doorway. "We've been monitoring Debbi Mitchell's work computer as part of an ongoing investigation. Our technicians have evidence that you illegally accessed and deleted files related to an open case of ours."

As realization dawned, cold tendrils of dread snaked down her spine.

"There's been a misunderstanding," she protested, fighting to keep her voice steady against the rising tide of panic. "I only deleted a personal file about me. It had nothing to do with any FBI investigation."

But Miles's razor-sharp features remained infuriatingly impassive, his mouth a flat line as he stared her down. "My forensic team seems to think otherwise when they recovered the file."

"Recovered?" Dolly's throat constricted so tightly she could barely force the words out. "You mean you've…you've seen…?"

"We've seen everything, Ms. Keller." There was no sympathy in Miles's tone, only an undisguised warning. "Which is why I need you to come with me."

"Do I need a lawyer?" she asked, not believing this was happening.

"That is your right to have one during questioning, but things don't have to get that official." He gestured toward his car. "We just want to record our interview with you."

"Let me just grab my purse and lock up," she said.

He nodded.

Leaving him on the doorstep, she went into her bedroom and shot off a quick text to Nash.

Miles Garrett from the FBI is taking me in for questioning. What should I do?

The text came back immediately. *Don't say anything until I get there.*

I don't know where he's taking me.

"Ms. Keller?" Miles called from the door. "Let's go."

I'll find out and meet you there.

Stuffing the phone into her purse, she hurried back out. "I'm coming."

After locking her apartment door, she got into the front seat of Miles's sedan. She fought the rising urge to hyperventilate as the car's engine rumbled to life. "This is just a misunderstanding," she said as Miles pulled away from the RV park.

But Miles remained stone-faced, refusing to engage any further until they arrived at a discreet mobile office tucked away in a vacant lot. He ushered Dolly inside the cramped trailer, bringing her to a sparsely furnished room with a folding table and chairs. "Please, have a seat Ms. Keller. Can I get you some coffee?"

Caught off guard by his bland politeness, Dolly could only nod mutely as Miles departed, leaving her to stew in dread and confusion. Finally, he returned with Styrofoam cups and settled across from her.

"Now then," he began crisply, "you expressed a desire to explain yourself regarding the files you deleted from Ms. Mitchell's computer. I'm listening."

Dolly wet her dry lips, throat tight with nerves.

"I…yes. Of course. You see, it wasn't anything related to your case. It was just a personal file. About me." *Where the hell are you, Nash?*

Miles's expression didn't flicker. "Why did you delete it?"

"You've seen what was in it, right?"

The trailer's door banged open before Miles could respond. Nash stormed inside with fire in his eyes.

"What the hell is going on here, Miles?" He looked poised for violence as Miles rose calmly to face him.

"Ms. Keller has some explaining to do."

"The hell she does," Nash snarled, moving to stand protectively beside Dolly. "You've got no right dragging her down here like a criminal."

"Actually, I do," Miles said evenly. "She deleted files off Debbi Mitchell's computer."

"You did what?" Nash whirled to her.

She flinched back from the incredulous look in his eyes.

"One file. I deleted one file, and it had nothing to do with the rodeo."

"Since she obviously called you instead of her lawyer, you might as well stay."

Nash looked mutinous, but after a beat, slid into the chair next to Dolly, taking her clammy hand in his larger, calloused one. His dark eyes searched her face. "You okay, sweetheart?" His voice was low, tense. Dolly squeezed his hand hard, drawing courage from his presence despite the fact this was not how she wanted to tell him about her escort days.

"Yeah."

Miles cleared his throat meaningfully as Nash reluctantly released Dolly's hand. "Let's start from the top. What can you tell me about your relationship with Jackson Blevins?"

"He's one of my bosses. He and Shelby Miller assign me marketing and promotion tasks."

"Are you having an affair with him?"

Nash stood up in his chair, squaring off against Miles.

Dolly yanked Nash back down. "No. Gross. He hates women and he's a real prick."

Miles blinked at her. "He gave you a cheerleading outfit from your professional days."

Dolly didn't like the way he said professional and based on the way Nash was gritting his teeth, he wasn't too thrilled about it either.

"I hadn't realized he had given me that gift. He left it anonymously."

"Gift?" Nash said. "That's the one you were so upset about?"

She nodded. "Sorry, I lied to you. I didn't know he had been the one to send it until later."

"Good thing he's already in the hospital," Nash muttered.

"What was in the file that you deleted?"

"You said you read it," she hedged. This was not how she wanted Nash to find out.

"Tell me anyway."

Squeezing Nash's hand in apology, she said, "It was a file about my previous job at a company called Leisure Industries. I was a…an escort for a brief time." She turned to Nash, whose face was strangely impassive. "I never slept with anyone for money. I had planned to, but I chickened out at the last minute. I'm not proud of what I did, but I learned from the experience. I wanted a fresh start, so I didn't disclose any of this on my application when I applied to the UPRC. They have a morality clause in their contract. I probably wouldn't have been hired if I had mentioned my time at Leisure—" She broke off. It was hard to breathe. Her chest hurt.

"You don't have to say anything else," Nash said.

"No. I want to. I need to. Anyway, when I saw that Blevins was the one who sent me the cheerleading outfit, I was afraid that he was planning on using my past to blackmail me."

"Blackmail you for what?" Miles said.

"To shake my pom poms," Dolly snapped. "I didn't want to give him the satisfaction. I've been documenting all the inappropriate things he does or says to me." She turned to Nash. "You can check that with Shelby—she knows and has been encouraging me to keep a log."

"Give me your phone," Miles demanded, his hand extended. "I need to check the messages."

Nash's fists clenched as he tried to intervene. "That's not necessary, Dolly. You don't owe him anything."

But she shook her head, determined to be transparent. "I don't want any more secrets." She handed her phone over to Miles. "Anyway, that's why I deleted the file."

"It probably wasn't the only copy," Nash said softly.

"Yeah." She gave a half-laugh. "Now that I've got a hot second to think about it, I see that it was a dumb move. I panicked."

"I need to make copies of these." Miles eyed Nash warily before leaving the room, her phone in his hand. The silence that followed was thick with tension.

It took every ounce of courage Dolly had to face Nash and confess the rest of her past. "I'm sorry I never told you about this," she said, her voice cracking. "I should've been honest from the start. But I was frightened and ashamed."

"It doesn't matter to me, Dolly," Nash replied, his eyes softening. "I always knew."

Her blue eyes widened in shock. "Who else knows?"

"Shelby."

The knowledge that someone she admired knew her secret made her feel exposed, vulnerable. She crossed her arms defensively, trying to shield herself from the weight of his gaze.

"When I started digging into Blevins and the UPRC, I did a deep background check on everyone involved, including you," he continued, his eyes never leaving hers. "And yes, you were one of my suspects at first. But like Shane and the Viking Ranch, it just didn't add up for you to be working with Blevins."

Anger flared within Dolly, her cheeks burning with indignation. "You knew, and you didn't say anything?"

Nash sighed, rubbing the back of his neck as he looked away. "I was waiting for you to tell me. I didn't want to pressure you or make you feel like you couldn't trust me with your secrets."

Her anger waned, replaced by a heavy sense of unease. "Do you believe me, Nash? That I never actually slept with anyone for money?" The words tasted bitter on her tongue, the admission of her past still feeling foreign and raw.

"I do," he said.

Dolly looked away, struggling to process the sincerity in his voice. Could she really trust him? Did he truly believe her, or was he just saying what he thought she needed to hear? She wanted desperately to believe him, to let his faith in her wash away the lingering shame and doubt that had plagued her for so long.

"Thank you," she whispered, not daring to meet his eyes. The words felt hollow, but they were all she had, a feeble attempt at acknowledging the depth of her gratitude and his unwavering support.

Miles returned, his stern expression softening as he addressed Dolly. "The bureau won't be pressing charges, provided you no longer interfere in the investigation. You're free to go," he said, handing back her phone.

Relief washed over her, but it did little to ease the tension that coiled in her gut.

"I appreciate that," she said, unable to keep the tremor from her voice.

Nash shot her a reassuring look before turning back to Miles. As they stood up, Miles gestured toward Nash. "A quick word in private?"

"I'll wait for you by your truck, Nash," Dolly said, trying to sound casual despite her wavering nerves. "You can give me a ride to work. I'm late."

As she walked out of the trailer, she caught sight of Debbi, looking miserable, in a meeting with another agent. Her mind raced with possibilities, and she wondered if they were getting closer to uncovering information on Blevins's offshore account.

Waiting outside, Dolly leaned against Nash's truck, feeling the warmth of the sun on her skin.

She glanced back at the trailer, curiosity gnawing at her insides. The arid breeze did little to lift the unease still churning within her. It wasn't every day a girl got grilled by the FBI as a suspect and lived to tell about it. What were Nash and Miles discussing? Was it about her, or something else related to the investigation?

"Ready to go?" Nash's voice startled her out of her reverie as he approached the truck.

"Y-yeah," she stuttered, trying to shake off her uncertainty. "Let's go."

As they drove away from the makeshift FBI headquarters, Dolly stole glances at Nash. His jaw was set, his eyes focused on the road ahead. Was he really okay with her past? She could prove it to him. She could call up Jefferson Laker and ask him to talk with Nash. It would be horribly unprofessional and a potential career-ending move, but if Nash had any doubts about her character, it would be worth it.

Chapter Nineteen

Nash

NASH WASN'T SURE how to address the elephant in the room—or rather the strained silence between them in his truck. He pulled into her apartment complex.

"I need to go to work," Dolly said.

"I told Shelby you were taking the day off."

"You had no right," Dolly began, but then trailed off. "Is she going to fire me?"

"What? No."

"But the morality clause…"

"She doesn't give a shit about that. The morality clause is there for people who try to do illegal things in the rodeo's name. Like our buddy Jackson Blevins. Can I come up?"

"Yeah," Dolly said and got out of the truck. Once they were in the apartment, Dolly said, "Can I get you anything?"

"Just this." He pulled her into his arms and kissed her. After a surprised moment, she hugged him tight and kissed him back. He would have loved to take this further, but he still had to tell her about Dr. Lance's statement, which was now being reviewed by the UPRC board. It was only a matter of time before his own morality clause bit him on the ass and he was ousted, leaving Shelby as the sole CEO.

Reluctantly, he broke off the kiss.

"So I didn't ruin things?" she asked.

He shook his head. "No."

"I was going to tell you last night. Loretta and I had a long talk. I was just so afraid you'd think less of me. I can call Jefferson Laker and you can talk with him."

"Who's Jefferson Laker?"

"Finn's father. He had hired me as an escort, but I couldn't go through with the sex part."

"I'm sure the last thing Jefferson wants to do is talk about hiring escorts with me."

Dolly stifled a chuckle. "Yeah, I guess you're right. But he can at least tell you I never went through with it. I never slept with anyone for money. He can vouch for me."

"You don't need to prove anything to me. The choices you made, the things you had to do to get where you are. I can only imagine the strength that took. The grit. I know you've worked your ass off to build yourself up from nothing. So don't sell yourself short. You've been through a lot, and you did your best. That's all anyone can ask for. You're strong. Stronger than you realize. And I'm proud of you."

"That means a lot."

"Even if you had been a full-service escort, it doesn't matter to me." He tilted up her chin so she could look into his eyes.

"But you're a rule guy and sleeping with people for money is illegal."

"I know. But maybe I'm learning that if it doesn't hurt someone else, it's sometimes okay to break a rule. You being an escort only hurt you. And I hate that. But at the end of the day, you were doing what you thought was right and what you had to do. That's none of my business, especially since it happened long before I met you."

"So you're really okay with this?"

Nash nodded. "I'm not okay that Jackson Blevins sent you that gift and got you upset."

"I'm sorry I didn't tell you."

"I understand why you didn't. But in the future..."

"You'll be the first one I come to."

"I'm going to hold you to that," he said. "And now it's my turn to tell you something about my past."

"Were you a hooker too?"

He gave a half-laugh. "No."

"Let's sit down," she said and sat next to him on the couch.

"Miles Garrett was my partner when we worked at the FBI. It ended badly between us."

"Badly how?"

"Miles wasn't following the rules. I reported him. More than once. He got his wrist slapped and then requested a transfer, which was granted. And I was encouraged to retire or get used to riding a desk."

"That doesn't seem fair," she said.

"It wasn't. So Miles and I have history and I'm having a hard time trusting him because of his past. I know the world isn't black and white, but operating in the gray still seems wrong to me."

"What's he investigating? Is it Blevins? He can't screw this up for us."

"Forget Blevins for a moment. He's a nonissue."

"How can you say that?" she asked, staring at him incredulously.

"Because this is more important. You and I are more important. I've spent so much time trying to pin something on Blevins, I missed out on a lot of opportunities. Opportunities to be with you." Nash stroked her hair. "I lost everything once because I couldn't compromise. I don't want to lose you too."

"Fat chance that's going to happen." Dolly took a deep breath. "I think I love you."

Nash wasn't sure he'd heard that correctly. "What?"

She slugged him in the arm. "Your turn." And then she looked more vulnerable than he ever wanted her to look.

"I'm falling in love with you too," he said.

"So, what now?" Dolly asked, looking like she was holding her breath.

"Maybe it's time we see where this goes," he said, his gaze never leaving hers.

"It's a relief, you know," she said. "That you know my past and you're okay with it. I've been so ashamed for so long, but maybe I can start forgiving myself."

"There's nothing to forgive." His free hand came up to cup her cheek, thumb brushing the corner of her mouth. Rational thought fled. All that remained was sensation. Need.

Nash felt the world slow down as their lips met, a tender, unhurried kiss that seemed to promise a future beyond the chaos of their present. Dolly's warmth seeped into him, grounding him even as his heart hammered in his chest. He lost himself in the taste of her, the softness of her lips against his, and the firm pressure of her body pressed to his. This was where he needed to be.

His tongue slipped past her lips, exploring with a hunger that mirrored his own longing. Dolly's moans, muffled by their kiss, vibrated against his mouth. Her hands roamed over his muscular back, pulling him closer, urging him on. She arched her back, pressing her breasts against his hard chest, and their mouths collided in a desperate frenzy of need and desire.

Nash let his lips trail down her neck. Dolly's fingers tangled in his hair, guiding him lower, a silent plea he was all too happy to answer.

"Nash," she gasped, her voice raw with want.

He didn't respond with words. Instead, he answered her with action. He pulled off her shirt and bra, and his mouth found her aching nipple, teasing it with his tongue. He sucked on the peak of her breast, feeling her quake beneath him. His hand roamed up her thigh, hiking up her skirt to find her panties already drenched with anticipation.

"I like how wet you are," he murmured against her skin.

His fingers slipped inside her panties, brushing against her swollen folds. Dolly's head fell back, her breath coming in short, ragged gasps as she clung to him.

"Right there," she moaned, her voice trembling.

Nash grinned wickedly, dipping his head to tease her other nipple with the same intensity. Her moans grew louder, and he reveled in the way her body responded to his touch. "You're perfect," he said, his voice raw with sincerity.

"Nash, I can't... I'm going to..." she panted.

He held her tighter, his fingers working her faster until she cried out his name, her body shuddering against his as her orgasm crashed over her. He soothed her with gentle kisses along her neck, holding her close as her tremors subsided.

"Shh, I got you," he whispered, his voice a soothing balm to her still-quivering form.

Dolly fumbled with the buckle of his belt, her need for him as urgent as his own. Nash's hands joined hers, quickly undoing the belt and tossing it aside. The sound of zippers and rustling fabric filled the air as they stripped off their clothes.

When they were finally naked, Dolly shivered, her eyes hungrily roaming over his body. Nash's gaze mirrored hers, taking in every curve, every inch of her. He could see the desire in her eyes, matching his own.

"Like what you see?" he asked, a playful edge to his voice.

"I think I'd like it better if you were inside me," she replied, her voice breathless.

"Your wish is my command." With a heated grunt, Nash scooped her up and carried her to the bed, lowering them both until they were entangled together. The sensation of their slick, heated skin sliding together sent shivers down his spine, and he couldn't stop himself from groaning in pleasure.

"God, Dolly," he said, his voice a mix of awe and desire. "You're gorgeous."

He stroked her body, playing her like an instrument. As his fingers danced over her, Dolly teetered on the edge of delirium. He kissed down her body, his stubble grazing her inner thighs as he nuzzled between them. His tongue flicked and licked, bringing her to another orgasm with steady strokes around her clit.

"Are you ready for me, sweetheart?" Nash asked, his words a heated whisper.

"Please," she begged. "I can't take it anymore. I want you more than anything."

He pinned her arms above her head and parted her legs with his thigh. Slowly, he eased inside her, the sensation drawing a blissful sigh from her. He held there for a moment, savoring the connection.

"Look at me," he said, brushing light kisses over her eyelids. "I want to see you come apart."

Dolly forced her eyes open, wrapping her legs around his waist. As they moved together, their passion cresting higher and higher, Nash lost himself in the torrent of sensation. He rocked into her faster, each thrust bringing them closer to the edge.

"More," she whispered, her voice filled with delight and need.

He gave it to her, driving them both to the brink and beyond. With each deep thrust, Dolly's past seemed to crumble away, leaving only the present, the intensity of their connection. She clung to him, nails digging into his back as wave after wave of pleasure cascaded over her.

Finally, as the last shudder of their climax subsided, they lay entwined, their breaths mingling. Nash brushed a stray tendril of hair from her cheek, his touch tender. He had a few moments of peaceful bliss and then she turned on her side and asked him, "What is Miles Garrett investigating?"

"First of all, Dr. Victor Lance wrote up a statement that Jackson Blevins threatened to kill him if he didn't dope up bulls. He said that Blevins was using enforcers to beat people up if they didn't do what he wanted."

"Is that enough?" Dolly asked, leaning up on her elbow.

"We'll find out. Shelby called an emergency board meeting."

"We got him," she said, squealing and hugging him.

"It looks like it."

"What if it's not enough?" she said, pulling back and biting her lip nervously.

"That's where Miles's investigation comes in. Hector Ortiz is an undercover agent. They think the Jaripeo Ranch is smuggling drugs into the States using the rodeo as a cover." Frustration simmered through him. "I should be on this case, not sitting on my thumbs waiting for scraps of intel. If I was still active…" He trailed off, shaking his head. "It's difficult, you know? Losing control over the investigation to Miles. Not being an agent anymore."

She rubbed his arm. "He's a bit of a prick. I'm glad you reported him."

Nash gave a half-laugh. "Didn't seem to harm his career any."

"Does he think Blevins knows about it?"

"It's Blevins's stock contractor. And Miles just told me that they found traces of cocaine in Blevins's office. I think it's a good bet that Blevins is done for. Financially, though, it's still a mess. Even if Shelby becomes the sole CEO, the rodeo's taken a huge loss in profit. It'll be a long climb back for the rodeo to get solvent and out of debt."

"So even if Blevins gets kicked out, the rodeo still could go under? That's not fair. Not at all."

"Yeah," Nash said quietly.

"That sucks." Dolly sat up, her sheet falling to her waist. "I can fix this. I can work on more promotions."

Nash yanked her back to the pillows. "This doesn't all fall on you. You're brilliant and you're a valued asset to the company. But you can't fix this alone and no one expects you to."

She was silent for a few more blissful moments and he considered starting up round two, but just as he was about to roll on top of her, she said, "What if we brought an investor on board? Someone with deep pockets who cares about keeping the rodeo alive?"

"Do you have someone in mind?" he asked, resigned to the fact that once Dolly got started, there wasn't any stopping her.

"Maybe Jefferson Laker."

Chapter Twenty

Dolly

Laredo, TX

DOLLY STOOD NEXT to Nash near the Jaripeo Ranch's enclosure, watching the Mexican fighting bulls snort and paw at the ground. Their broad backs rippled with muscle, each of the ten bulls a coiled spring of aggression. The wranglers had their hands full keeping them watered and fed until it was time to bring them to the chute.

"I thought the FBI was going to have Jaripeo Ranch's trailer wrapped in crime scene tape by now," Dolly muttered, eyeing the restless animals warily.

"Looks like they came up empty," Nash said. "Miles hasn't answered my texts either."

"At least we don't have to worry if Jackson Blevins will scoot out of this."

Shelby got a unanimous vote of "no confidence" against Jackson Blevins. He was out of a job and out of luck. His things were being packed up and would be waiting for him at the reception area in the Dallas headquarters once he left the hospital.

"I mentioned Jefferson Laker to Shelby as a potential

investor. She's considering it."

"Will working with him be a problem for you?" Nash asked, a flash of concern on his face.

"Not anymore." And she meant it. The people who needed to know about her past, knew it. She wasn't going to worry about her secret getting out.

He reached down to hold her hand. "Good."

One of the bulls charged the fence, testing its strength. Dolly grimaced. "I bet you're glad you don't have to ride any of these monsters. Your undercover cowboy days are over."

"I think I might actually miss it."

"Really?" She cocked her head up at him.

The corner of his eyes crinkled as he smiled. "Nope. I lied."

"Nash Weaver, I'm shocked."

Two kids who were standing close to them, approached them excitedly.

"Are you Nash Weaver?" one asked.

He nodded, trying to mask his discomfort at the sudden attention. "Yeah, that's me."

"Can we take a picture with you and Donnan?" the other chimed in, practically bouncing on the spot.

Dolly hid her delighted grin behind her hand as Nash agreed, leading them over to the petting zoo where a crowd of young fans eagerly waited. The moment he appeared, they swarmed him, clamoring for autographs and photos.

"I forgot to tell you," Dolly said, her voice barely audible above the excited chatter. "Your posts with Donnan have gone viral these last few days. You're trending."

Dolly watched Nash blink in surprise, clearly overwhelmed by the sudden appreciation for him and his furry little friend. A rodeo star—him. It was ironic, considering he wasn't any good at bull riding. Yet, here he was, signing hats and posing for selfies, almost basking in the glow of his unintended fame. And the best part? He didn't have to get tossed on his ass today.

"Guess I'll leave bull riding to the professionals," Nash said.

"Good. I've got enough on my plate without worrying about you getting gored by one of those things." She glanced at her phone, then back at him. "There are more kids coming to see Donnan. You might want to take a breather and sneak away for a bit. Let's go around the back area."

They slipped behind the petting zoo toward the animal trailers, expecting a moment of solitude and maybe a little private kissing time. Instead, she did a double take when she spotted two familiar goons—the ones from Blevins's office security footage—engrossed in conversation with Ryan Chester from Rocky Ridge Ranch. Nash pulled her behind a nearby trailer with him.

Dolly, camera in hand, snapped several quick photos, capturing the exchange of thick wads of cash between the men. Nash turned on the recorder on his cell phone, boosting the signal to catch every word.

"...Blevins won't know the actual amounts delivered," Ryan was saying, his voice dripping with contempt. "He's in the hospital for a few more days. Man, he loves his powder more than his profits."

"We should just cut him out altogether," one of the goons said.

They watched from their hiding spot as the three men moved away. After they disappeared into the bustle of the rodeo, Nash let out a deep sigh and sagged against the trailer.

"Holy shit. We nailed him. I've got to let Miles know it wasn't the Jaripeo Ranch; it was Rocky Ridge that was smuggling."

She watched as he texted: *Wrong border. It was coming in from Canada, not Mexico. Check the pics and recording I'm sending.* He attached the pictures and audio clip and hit send.

"We should get out of here and let the FBI do their job," Dolly said, with her hand on his arm.

Nash looked wistfully in the direction where the three men had gone. After a moment, he nodded. "Yeah, you're right."

Nash

DOLLY'S FINGERS PLAYED with the edge of the popcorn box as she scanned the arena. The stands were packed, spectators buzzing for that wild rodeo action. The smell of sawdust and leather mixed with the salty scent of popcorn. Nash, next to her, grabbed a handful of popcorn, his eyes on the dirt track where cowboys and cowgirls showed off their skills. It was no surprise that Finn took first place in bull riding, but Taylor Keating coming in second? That was a shock.

"Do you think Loretta saw?" Dolly asked, stretching to see if her sister was in the crowd.

"I think she was too busy selling paintings," Nash replied.

Nash's phone buzzed. He glanced down and saw a text from Miles. *Got 'em. I owe you one. I'll be in touch.*

Nash laughed quietly. He thought about his old life at the bureau, when following the rules to the letter had been everything to him. But looking at Dolly smiling up at him, he knew he had everything he needed right here. He wrapped an arm around her shoulders, pulling her closer.

Just then, his phone rang again. Shelby's name lit up the screen. Nash answered, hoping for good news.

"The FBI found drugs in sealed containers in the Rocky Ridge Ranch trailers under the dirty hay," Shelby said loud enough for Dolly to hear. Dolly leaned in closer.

"They were hiding it under cow shit?" Dolly said, eyebrows raised.

"Apparently, one of the cows stepped on a container and shattered it. We almost had a cocaine cow at the petting zoo." Shelby's voice had a dark humor to it.

"What'll happen to the petting zoo animals?" Nash asked, glancing at Dolly.

"Most of the smaller ones have temporary homes, but Donnan and his mother are going to be impounded."

"Let me handle this," Dolly said, taking out her phone and calling her sister Reba.

"Reba, can you convince Shane to keep Donnan and

his mother at the Viking Ranch? They've got plenty of room, right?"

"Wait!" Nash heard Reba screech. "You won't adopt a kitten for me, but you want me to take in two cows?"

"Please, Reba? They're going to be impounded if you don't."

Nash heard some grumbling, but eventually, Reba agreed to take in the Highland cows.

Dolly leaned her head on Nash's shoulder.

"So, now that you've stopped a drug-smuggling operation and ousted Blevins as co-CEO, what's next?" she asked.

"Maybe I'll set up a private investigation office in Dallas," Nash said with a smile.

"Really?" Dolly's eyes sparkled with excitement. "I think that's a great idea. Maybe I could help with the social media side of things?"

"We make a good team."

"We do. And you know what?" Dolly said playfully. "You can still be a rodeo cowboy on weekends."

"I'm not so sure about that."

"There's got to be something you're good at."

"Gee, thanks," he said dryly.

"I mean, you can't rely on Donnan for your whole career," Dolly teased, snuggling closer. Nash kissed her hair, breathing in her floral scent. She was all he needed. Anything else would just be the cherry on top of the sundae.

Epilogue

LORETTA PACED THE narrow aisle of the Winnebago, each step a testament to her frayed nerves. She chewed on her thumbnail, a bad habit from childhood that resurfaced whenever she was upset. Pausing at the small kitchenette, she wondered if she should make herself something to eat, although the thought of food turned her stomach at the moment. The hum of the refrigerator served as a monotonous soundtrack to her swirling thoughts.

A text buzzed in and she spared a glance at her phone. It was Dolly telling her that she had the Winnebago all to herself tonight because she was spending the night with Nash setting up his new PI office in Dallas.

Is that what they're calling it these days? she texted back, a bubble of happiness for her sister soothing some of the anxiety in her gut.

All of Loretta's sisters were coupling up and settling down—Dolly with Nash, Reba with Shane, LeAnn with Dylan. Meanwhile, Loretta's love life was a mess of epic proportions.

She winced, remembering walking in on her rock star husband tangled up naked with a groupie, every bit the cliché with his infidelities strewn across tabloids like dirty

211

laundry. Then there was her art professor she'd had an ill-advised affair with, who'd conveniently failed to mention his wife and kids. Loretta snorted. She sure could pick them.

Then her thoughts drifted to Taylor Keating, the bull rider slash bullfighter she'd been seeing recently. With his easy smile and gentlemanly ways, he was so different from the self-absorbed cheaters of her past. What they had together felt real, meaningful. Like it could turn into something serious, something lasting.

Except this could change everything.

In the next few minutes, everything between her and Taylor could change irrevocably. Her hand drifted unconsciously to her still-flat belly as a wave of nervous anticipation crested inside her. One little plastic stick could rewrite their entire future, for better or worse.

Loretta stared down at the pregnancy test clutched in her trembling hand, squinting at the tiny window in disbelief. Was that one line or two? The plastic edges dug into her palm as she tightened her grip, willing the results to resolve into focus.

A sharp knock at the Winnebago door jolted her out of her spiraling thoughts and Taylor walked in carrying a bouquet of wildflowers. His eyes widened when he saw what she was holding.

"Hey," he said, his voice laced with surprise.

"Hey," she said back and put the test on the table. It still wasn't time for a conclusive result.

He handed her the flowers mechanically. "Is that…"

She nodded, the lump in her throat making it impossible to speak.

"Wow," he said softly, thumbing a tear that threatened to escape the corner of her eye. "Whatever happens, I'm here for you."

Her stomach twisted with uncertainty. "What if I choose to keep it?"

"Then I'd be honored to be a daddy," he replied, his voice steady.

"You don't have to marry me," she said, trying to keep her voice level.

"I wouldn't," he replied, "not unless we both knew it was right." The honesty in his voice chipped away at the walls she'd built around her heart after too many betrayals.

"If I'm pregnant, I want to keep it." She watched for any flinch, any sign of regret.

Taylor nodded slowly. "I'd love that too. And I'd be there, every step of the way. For you and the little one."

The sincerity in his voice wrapped around her like a warm quilt, easing the tight coil of anxiety in her gut. Maybe, just maybe, they could navigate this unexpected path together. Find a way to make it work.

She took a fortifying breath. "Okay. Okay, good." The possibility of not being alone in this softened something inside her, eased a tension she hadn't realized she was holding. "But what if I'm not?" The question slipped out, exposing her raw need for reassurance.

He huffed a rueful chuckle. "Well, for starters, we'll be damn sure to stock up on protection from now on."

A surprised giggle bubbled out of her, laced with an edge of hysteria. The absurdity of the situation crashed over her in a dizzying wave.

"Tell you what," Taylor continued, eyes crinkling at the corners, "if that test comes back negative, I'm taking you out on the town. We'll hit up the swankiest club, get bottle service in the VIP lounge, and drink and dance till dawn. What do you say?"

The image drew a genuine smile from her, the idea of recklessness with him a balm to the fear that had tightened around her chest. It sounded good, sounded like a sliver of normalcy she didn't realize she craved. "I say you've got yourself a deal, cowboy."

Loretta twirled the pregnancy test between her fingers, the tiny plastic object suddenly the fulcrum of her world. Taylor stood close, his presence a warm blanket around her shoulders. She glanced up at him, his eyes steady and encouraging, and with a deep breath that did little to still her racing heart, she looked down at the result.

The End

Read all about it in *Christmas Baby for the Cowboy*.

If you enjoyed *The Undercover Cowboy*,
check out the other books in the

Sweethearts of the Rodeo series

Book 1: *The Cowboy's Prize*

Book 2: *The Cowboy's Untamed Heart*

Book 3: *The Undercover Cowboy*

Book 4: *Christmas Baby for the Cowboy*

Available now at your favorite online retailer!

More books by Jamie K. Schmidt

Three Sisters Ranch series

Book 1: *The Cowboy's Daughter*
Book 2: *The Cowboy's Hunt*
Book 3: *The Cowboy's Heart*
Book 4: *A Cowboy for April*
Book 5: *A Cowboy for June*
Book 6: *A Cowboy for Merry*

Other Titles

A Spark of Romance
Summer Lovin: A Sweet Romance Anthology

Available now at your favorite online retailer!

About the Author

USA Today bestselling author, Jamie K. Schmidt, writes erotic contemporary love stories and paranormal romances. Her steamy, romantic comedy, Life's a Beach, reached #65 on USA Today, #2 on Barnes & Noble and #9 on Amazon and iBooks. Her Club Inferno series from Random House's Loveswept line has hit both the Amazon and Barnes & Noble top one hundred lists. The first book in the series, Heat, put her on the USA Today bestseller list for the first time, and is a #1 Amazon bestseller. Her book Stud is a 2018 Romance Writers of America Rita® Finalist in Erotica. Her dragon paranormal romance series has been called "fun and quirky" and "endearing." Partnered with New York Times bestselling author and former porn actress, Jenna Jameson, Jamie's hardcover debut, SPICE, continues Jenna's FATE trilogy.

Thank you for reading

The Undercover Cowboy

If you enjoyed this book, you can find more from all our great authors at TulePublishing.com, or from your favorite online retailer.

Printed in Great Britain
by Amazon

47819155R00128